Cotton and Candlelight

A Douglas Powell,
Casey Malone Story

BY

B. BENEDICT BRADDOCK

This is a work of fiction. The events and characters described herein are imaginary and are not intended to refer to any real places or persons living or deceased.

Please contact the publisher:

Empathy Books

Humanservicesconsultants@gmail.com

Empathy Books

Book One: The Common Life of Casey Malone

Book Two: Cotton and Candlelight

Book Design and Cover by *Usama Bajwa.*

E-mail: usamabajwa040@gmail.com

Table of Contents

Week One

"You want your eggs scrambled?" Douglas called over his shoulder.

"That's the only way you know how to make them," Casey laughed.

"I can do a decent over-easy."

"No, you can't."

He grinned and went about the task of whisking, pouring and carefully watching over the eggs as they began to heat up in the pan.

"You have class today?"

"Two", she shouted back from her room. "Contemporary Lit and Sociology."

"Gosh, rough day for you."

"Yeah, and two papers due by next Friday," she said as she came into the kitchen area and pulled up a stool to watch him plate the eggs, English muffins and apple slices.

"Yikes. I guess not much socializing for you this week."

"Yeah, like I'm out partying the rest of the time."

It had been just over a year since Casey Malone had walked out of the Georgia Women's Reception Center and accepted Douglas Powell's offer to move into his spare bedroom. During that time she had completed her High School program, enrolled in community college, and religiously engaged in therapy with a counselor whom she liked and respected. The road had been and still was hard at times, but the results had been as tremendous as Douglas had hoped. When she was home he would find her either doing school assignments or engaging her addiction to everything gothic, dark, and supernatural that the fiction world had to offer. She wanted to be a writer, and what better training than to read the work of others who'd been a success.

About ten hours per week Casey would earn her two-hundred dollar per week paycheck from the Atlanta Daily News assisting Douglas as his personal assistant. Since her own story had propelled the Daily's ever-growing popularity and sales, the executives had not batted an eye at putting her on the payroll. Besides, the testing that had been ordered by Casey's therapist proved what Douglas had already known. Casey had an above average I.Q. and was worth her weight in editing gold. She left very little for the main office staff to do and could skim through a document and find mistakes in half the average time. If the young lady was going to be a writer, they were going to scoop her up themselves. Perhaps, Douglas had already suggested, to fill his spot when he retired.

Douglas had become like a father to Casey, teaching her first to drive and use her new i-phone and then everything he could about becoming a successful and happy adult. She was twenty years old now, strong, capable and already tested. Her spirit and her wit had never been taken from her and her imagination was bright and hopeful. She had two years left of community college and then would go on for a Bachelor degree in English Literature. Her own choice. The fact that she was seeming to follow in his footsteps was not lost on him, and he found himself both proud and humbled.

"Where are you off to today?" Casey asked over a forkful of eggs.

"Well, we got a call from the parents of a kid named Jeremy Timmons. They're saying that their son committed suicide after being bullied non-stop for being gay. They complained to the school and the Board of education but nothing was ever done and they want them held responsible for the tragedy."

"Where'd he go to school?"

"Jefferson High, about forty minutes out into the country."

"Boy, you just can't seem to be able to pull away from the High School scene."

"Right," he smiled. "It's my expertise now."

"And Sammy knows it, too."

"Don't laugh. She said it was right up my alley and I should take Malone with me."

"Ha. No thanks. I've had quite enough of High School Sir."

"I figured."

A knock sounded at the door and Casey got up to answer it. Lloyd McAfee stood in the hallway holding a cardboard coffee cup carrier with three large cups. "Malone."

"McAfee."

She stood aside and let him enter.

"I gotta say Powell, every time I come I'm surprised to see that Malone hasn't whacked you out yet."

"And I'm surprised you can find your own pee pee under that gigantic belly," she countered. "Give me my coffee."

McAfee grinned and handed her one of the cups. "You're still a smart ass Malone."

"Yup. And you're still, well, you."

4

"Everybody loves me."

"I'm sure."

McAfee pulled up a stool and pulled the lid off of his own cup.

"You want eggs?" Douglas asked him.

"Nah, I'm good."

Lloyd McAfee had retired from the Atlanta PD major crimes division only six months earlier and got himself a Private Investigator license. He'd been almost immediately busy with a reputation for getting to the truth and being afraid of absolutely no one. He had been hired on several times to help Douglas with particularly intense investigations into corruption and organized crime and was tagging along for the day just to get out of the city.

"What time do you have to leave?" Casey asked.

Douglas checked his watch. "Right now, if you're sure you're not hungry Lloyd? Hopefully I beat the rush hour traffic."

McAfee waved his hand.

"Go. I'll get the dishes." Casey offered.

He threw on his sport- coat and gave her a wink. "You're the best."

"Thanks for breakfast."

"Try not to murder anyone today Malone," McAfee said as he stood back up.

"And you try not to get any donut jelly on that new tie pops."

Douglas grinned. Do you two need to hug it out?"

They both smirked. "I think we're good," Casey answered. "I'm not looking to get smothered this morning."

The ride up to Jefferson wasn't bad at all. They took the highway northwest then hoped on ninety-two for five miles or so which turned into Main Street, Jefferson. A sign greeted them announcing Jefferson as the Apple fritter capital of America.

"We're getting some of those bad boys 'fore we leave," McAfee mumbled.

"You're gonna have a damn heart attack," Douglas answered as he checked the GPS.

"You've been telling me that for years and I'm still here."

"Looks like it's only a couple of miles to the Timmons place."

"So tell me again what their complaint is."

"They haven't told me very much yet, but the gist of it is that their fourteen year old son, Jeremy, was horribly bullied for being gay. Not just by his classmates but apparently around town as well. There's what they call an environment of hate in the town. The poor kid took it on a daily basis until he'd finally had enough and took his own life."

McAfee shook his head. "When you're that age you can't even envision that things will ever change I guess."

"It's disgusting that a child that young is suffering enough to choose death. It's been happening more and more often. The question is whether the school and the department of education are at fault at all."

"They talk to a lawyer?"

"Not sure. But they damn well should."

Jefferson was a small community that hadn't changed all that much over the past sixty or so years. The original barber shop and Diner were still in operation and other than some newer gas pumps not a whole lot had ever been updated. There were only about two thousand residents in the town with many of the same families having been there for generations. They survived mostly on cotton, the second largest row crop in Georgia, and the town was surrounded by fields as far as you could see in any direction.

Douglas made a right hand turn just outside of downtown and headed out through a sea of the white stuff.

"It's October eleventh," McAfee said. "They'll be harvesting soon."

"Yup. And it's still hot as hell, poor bastards."

"I couldn't do it. You ever try picking some?"

"Yeah, field trip as a kid to one of the plantations. It was a good lesson in the suffering my family endured in the past."

"It's backbreaking for sure and it can tear the shit outta your hands if you aren't real careful."

"Well, most of the large crops are handled by machine now."

"Yeah but there's still plenty of Mom and Pop operations out there."

"Yup, peanuts too."

"We gotta stop for some boiled peanuts on the way back down."

Douglas shook his head. "Seriously Lloyd, try to make it through at least your first year of retirement before dropping dead."

"Peanuts are good for you."

"Sprinkled on top of your fritters right?"

"That sounds damn good. Thanks for the tip."

The road twisted and swerved, climbing hills and dropping back down into beautiful valleys that appeared to be covered in snow from atop the peak but proved to be bright white cotton once back down below. They were only ten minutes outside of town but the houses became sparse, with only the occasional barn dotting the landscape. The sun shone brightly over the fields creating a truly heavenly portrait. First impressions were peaceful ones but Douglas knew that first impressions were often very wrong.

"So when you gonna pull the plug?" McAfee asked.

"Retire? I don't know. I could go out if I wanted to but I love what I do. I could really do another fifteen and go to full retirement age."

"Damn, fifteen more?"

"You mean to tell me you don't miss the job just a little?"

"Sure, but shit. Not enough to push that far."

"It's different for cops though. You can't be out tackling guys at seventy."

"No. The guys that stay that long go on a desk. I'd rather die of an apple fritter overdose."

They pulled up in front of a long dirt driveway and stopped. The beat up old mailbox had the name Timmons painted on it.

"This is us," Douglas said.

"So, what's your angle?"

"I'm just gonna listen and hear them out for starters. Let's see if there's anything here that we can actually work with."

"Okay. I'll take some notes for you."

"Oh, that would be great, thanks."

"I'm just messing with you. I ain't doing shit."

Douglas smirked. "You're such an ass."

"Yup, can't deny it."

They pulled up the drive and came to a stop in front of an older farmhouse. It was actually in pretty good shape, Douglas thought, painted bright white with charcoal shutters and a nicely shaded wrap around porch that Southerner's craved. There was a small bit of lawn, a barn and tool shed, surrounded by nothing but cotton.

"Looks nice." he commented

"I'd lose my shit out here. I wonder if we even have reception." McAfee checked his phone. "Barely."

"Imagine this place a hundred years back."

"I guarantee you it was exactly the same."

They climbed out of the car and pulled on their suit jackets. It was warm, in the mid-eighties, and they both silently hoped that the house had been updated with central air conditioning. The screen door opened and a middle aged woman in jeans and a long sleeved white blouse stepped onto the porch. She was fortyish, rather attractive with long, dark hair and a welcoming smile.

"Y'all must be the gentlemen from the paper."

"Yes Ma'am," Douglas stepped forward. "Douglas Powell and Detective Lloyd McAfee."

Lloyd nodded and she smiled again. "I have some nice cold lemonade waiting on you. It's nice and cool inside so y'all come on in."

The home was warmly decorated in what Douglas assumed were heirloom antiques, with overstuffed chairs, quilts, and gorgeous rugs over hundred year old pine floors. There was a fireplace that he thought must be absolutely awesome when the weather turned colder.

They took seats around the coffee table as Mrs. Timmons placed a tray of cookies and two tall glasses of lemonade in front of them. She had just taken her own seat when they heard the back door open and Mister Timmons came into the living room to join them. "Hope I didn't keep y'all waiting too long." Douglas and Lloyd stood to shake his hand. "Time gets away from you out there."

"You about ready for harvest?" Douglas asked.

"Oh yeah, we'll start next week. It's been crazy around here lately and will be straight through till Christmas."

"You bring in extra help?"

"Some. Smaller growers like me are just better off partnering with larger companies that have the newest equipment. The costs can be phenomenal to buy your own."

They politely ate a cookie and sipped their drinks as they made some initial small-talk. The Timmons family had owned the land for three generations and had been in the Jefferson area for five. They had only one surviving child, a fourteen year old daughter named Emily.

"Do either of you have children?" Mrs. Timmons asked.

"Two daughters," Douglas answered.

""Two boys and a girl," McAfee said. "All grown and moved away now."

"Are yours at home Mister Powell?"

"Only one, she's a first year college student."

"Oh how nice."

"So Mister and Mrs. Timmons, would you like to tell me a bit about Jeremy?"

"He and Emily were twins," she began. "Not too much alike but they got along just fine. They both started High School back in August but the problems began long before that. Things just seemed to escalate quickly and Jeremy...." Her voice broke and she stopped for a moment to compose herself. Her husband reached over and grabbed her hand.

"Jeremy just fell apart," she managed to finish.

"Did he have many friends?" Douglas asked.

"Not really," Mister Timmons answered. "He came out as gay in the eighth grade and you know how things can go in a small town like this. There are only about a thousand kids total in our small school system and they all pretty much fall into line with what the popular kids say."

"You mean the bullies," McAfee offered.

"Exactly right. Emily tried to shield him a bit but then they started to stay away from her too."

"And now?" Douglas asked. "Has she been alright lately?"

"They've laid off a little since Jeremy….since last month."

"So he was only a month or so into High School when he passed?"

"Almost a month on the nose."

"I'm sorry to have to ask," McAfee said. "Can you tell us how it happened and was he here at home?"

"No, not here," Mrs. Timmons answered. "Just a ways down the road in a run down barn that hasn't been used in years. He….umm."

"He hung himself," her husband finished for her.

"We're so very sorry," Douglas offered."

Mister Timmons nodded. "Thank you. But what we really wanted to talk with you about is the fact that our son was driven to this by a bunch of punk kids right under the noses of the school officials and even the teachers. The popular kids run the show and the others are tormented."

"Like your son," McAfee said.

"Yes, Like our Jeremy," Misses Timmons answered. " He was just a kid, not even in a relationship, not forcing his way of life on anybody else. Just because he won't lie and deny who he is on the inside they berated him horribly, called him names, shoved him around, threatened him, excluded him. The kids were horrendous but they get it from their parents."

"The climate of hate you spoke of on the phone," Douglas nodded.

"Yes Sir. I have to tell you Mister Powell, you will meet with resistance yourself here as a black man. I just want to warn you that if you do decide to check around you'll need to be really careful."

Mrs. Timmons went to find a family photo album and show them some pictures of their son.

"Tell me who's who?" McAfee asked. "Who are the guys behind this climate of hate?" He took out his pad and waited.

"Well Sir," Mister Timmons answered. "There's Ted Larson, he's a local barber who is the leader of it all really. He's got a shop right there on Main where they all hang around and organize whatever they may be up to. Dexter Smith owns the grocery store right down the way from there. And Wille Charles is the Chief of Police. They're the main force behind it all but the Mayor, Tom Deen, all the school board members, the fire department, nearly everybody is involved."

"You're telling me a cop is wrapped up in this nonsense?" McAfee asked.

"Yessir. And all the other cops that work for him. We have eight in total."

Mrs. Timmons came back into the living room with the photo album and sat down between Douglas and Lloyd. She was obviously quite proud of her family but smiled rather sadly as she pointed out photos of her son.

"He loved art. He would spend hours outside, under the tree in the backyard, just drawing and drawing. He'd fill up sketch pads in less than a week sometimes. Sketch out his ideas first and then paint wonderful watercolors up in his room. Music too, he played the clarinet but he just couldn't get enough of Country music. He'd sing along so happy as he painted. Seemed like he didn't have a care in the world.

"But he did," Douglas said.

"Yes. Yes that's the truth of it."

"So he played in the band?"

"He did. Of course he just joined the High School orchestra this year but he used to play Christmas concerts and such in Junior High."

"Any other clubs, groups, sports?"

"No, just the music and art class of course."

McAfee continued to look through the photos. Jeremy and Emily as babies, elementary school kids, eight grade graduation, their fourteenth birthday. They looked well cared for, perfectly happy. He found some of their first day of High School. Emily posing in her flower dress, trying to look grown up. Jeremy in striped polo and khaki shorts. Smiling for his Mom but looking nervous for sure.

He took out his phone. "May I?"

"Yes, of course," Mrs. Timmons answered.

McAfee took photos of the latest pictures of Jeremy and one of the whole family.

"So the school and the board of education?" Douglas continued.

"We tried with them all," Mister Timmons answered. "The kids were brutal to him right from the start and it had never been that bad before."

"He came out as gay in eighth grade?"

"Yes, just toward the end of the school year. Pressure to ask a girl to the Junior High dance and all that. I think the poor boy just wanted to be at peace and be himself."

"So there wasn't much time for a reaction at the end of the year. It was all pent up and waiting to be unleashed on him the following year in ninth grade."

"Yessir. Exactly right."

"So the school?"

"They didn't pay us very much mind at all. Told us they would keep an eye out and that was about it. Six times in four weeks we talked to folks at the High School. The Lord only knows how many times we were at the Junior High the year before. Twice to people at the School Board."

"And what'd they say?"

"Not a thing. They would send out an email to the Principal and monitor the situation. They did nothing."

"Who's the High School Principal?

"Margaret Lawson."

Douglas checked his notes. "As in related to Ted Larson? The barber who bosses everyone around?"

"His wife. Yessir."

Douglas and Lloyd climbed back into the car. It had been sitting in the Sun for nearly an hour and a half and was stifling inside. Douglas cranked up the air.

"What do you think?" he asked.

"This is small- town, deep south, Powell. None of this is unusual. I don't see anything criminal right off the bat but people have been sent up for harassing someone to the point of suicide. We'd have to see who we're looking at here."

"There was certainly a plan to bully him. We'd have to know exactly what was said to determine if they actually intended to drive him to suicide."

"In a small town like this, we ain't gonna find any kids willing to talk."

"So what's our first move do you think?"

"I think I feel like a haircut. You?"

"They're not touching me brother. But I'm all for seeing some reaction to our visit. Let's stop down the street and take a look at the Barn where he died first. Snap a couple photos."

It was only half a mile from the Timmons home, an easy walking distance. It looked to be halfway between barn and tool shed, not overly big but more likely used for storage. It had seen better years for sure, not completely falling down but hardly in shape to be of much use anymore. It sat in the middle of the sea of endless white, on its own gravel road that'd been overgrown with weeds. The property was owned by the Jessler family, the immediate neighbors and friends of the Timmons clan who had given permission for the visit. Douglas parked the car and the men climbed out to survey the area.

"Lonely place," Douglas observed.

"I'm sure it felt that way to him," McAfee answered.

"I can't even imagine the pain that drove him to it."

"And at only fourteen."

They opened the dilapidated door, barely hanging on to its old hinges, and entered the barn. It seemed bigger inside than it did from the driveway, with a high beamed ceiling and one center cross beam that they assumed was where he'd killed himself. There was only a dirt floor, perhaps it had always been such, and sunlight streamed through the many open spaces between wallboards and holes in the roof. There was a loft and an old ladder, far from safe looking, that they assumed Jeremy had used to fasten the rope. Some bouquets of flowers had been left, now dead, and a teddy bear sat alone holding a photo of Jeremy.

"So, he's taken all that he possibly can, makes the decision to put an end to it, walks himself down here, uses the old ladder to fix the rope…" Douglas said.

"Does he bring the rope with him? Is it already here?" McAfee asks.

"Good question. And where'd he learn to tie the noose? Online? Did he hint at it to anyone?"

"His Dad said there was no note."

"But was there any indication? If so do they feel guilty and they won't tell us?"

"Coroner ruled it a suicide."

"You mean the probably corrupt buddy of the Chief of Police and the wannabe gangster barber?"

"Right. So we wanna check it all out ourselves. Investigate the death and the cause."

"I think so. But hell, he's been dead for a month now. If the Coroner is dirty then the report is useless."

"You think there's a chance he was helped up onto that beam?"

"I don't know. We do know he was most likely an emotional wreck dealing with all that he had over the past year. So did he do it? Probably. But let's have a talk with some of the kids and try to figure out what's what and who's who."

Larson's Barber shop was like a snapshot of small town America. The original Barber pole was still outside the door and the front picture window was lettered in red, white and blue, advertising men's cuts for only seven dollars. One of Main street's many benches rested directly under the window where a couple of elderly men now sat.

Douglas pulled his Mercedes to the curb in front of the shop, and the men followed him and McAfee with their eyes as they entered the storefront. Whatever conversation had been taking place came to an abrupt halt as they entered and McAfee removed his suit jacket, exposing his shoulder holster and Glock pistol. He hung it on a hook and turned to face the men as Douglas took a seat.

"Fella's."

There were five of them, three of them lounging in the barber chairs, two of them were obviously not barbers, and two others seated in the chairs used for waiting customers. One of the men was wearing a Barber coat and he stood up and smiled. "Gentlemen, how're y'all today?"

"Fine as can be expected," McAfee answered. "Just looking for a cut."

"Well, you're in the right place my friend. Don't recognize you. Y'all from around here?"

McAfee climbed into the chair and the barber wrapped an apron around him.

"Atlanta."

"That so? What brings you up from the city?"

"Visiting. Matter of fact he recommended your shop. Marty Timmons."

He hesitated but only for a second. "Why sure, Marty. How's the Ol' boy doin'?"

"Well, you know. With the tragedy and all."

"A damn shame," he nodded as he started to spray McAfee's hair to trim it. "Nobody should have to lose a child like that."

"Nope, that's the truth. We hear tell though that he was pushed into it."

"Pushed?"

"Yep. Bullied, Pressured, taunted."

"I'll be damned. First I heard that."

"It's horrible. You know how people are. They don't like to talk. But they'll talk to me."

"Well, folks kinda keep to themselves around here."

"Sure, sure. But still, if he was bullied into it, that's a crime. And if a crime happened, Imma find out."

"So you're police officers?"

"Just retired. Private Investigator now but with the entire State of Georgia law enforcement community behind me."

One of the other men smirked and McAfee spotted it in the mirror. He held up his hand for the Barber to stop cutting and swiveled his chair around to look at him.

"I say something that amused you Son?"

The man shrugged but said nothing. The Barber patted McAfee's shoulder. "He don't mean nuthin' Sir."

McAfee swung back around.

There was a tense silence for a moment until the Barber spoke again. "Name's Ted Lawson by the way."

"Lloyd McAfee. My partner Douglas Powell."

"Gentlemen," he nodded. "Powell, you the boy that got the little girl outta prison?"

Douglas glared at him. "I haven't been a boy in many years."

"No, no. Course not. Just a Southern expression buddy. No offense."

"So, how about telling us what you know about Jeremy Timmons," McAfee said.

"Not much to tell. He was a quiet kid, timid, more like a girl than a boy. Announced to the whole world that he went that way. You know, queer."

"So did he receive much support?"

"Of course not. That shit's a goddamn abomination. This ain't Los Angeles or somethin'."

"So he was bullied?"

"I didn't say that. I never heard nothing like that at all. Folks just didn't want him around them and they have that right. Nobody wants to encourage that kind of unnatural behavior."

"Big difference between distancing yourself and imposing your views."

"I wouldn't know nuthin' 'bout that. As far as I know the boy just didn't wanna live with that sickness the rest of his life."

They were back in the car and half a block away before Douglas spoke. "I feel like I need a damn shower."

"Yeah, they're some hateful fuckers for sure."

"He was only fourteen."

"I know it. Just stay focused and follow the facts Powell. Emotion only gets in the way."

They passed a Dairy Queen and McAfee insisted on stopping for a cone. As they waited at the window they noticed more and more teenagers arriving in vehicles, on bicycles or on foot.

"Lots of kids," Douglas commented to the girl working the window.

"High School just let out. They come here every day."

She went back to grab Douglas a Vanilla shake as McAfee started on his pecan cone.

"These kids could tell us plenty I bet," Douglas said.

"They won't tell us jack shit."

"Nope. But I know a cute somebody that they might tell it to."

McAfee smiled. "And she loves her some Dairy Queen don't she?"

"Y'all want me to do what?"

"It's no big deal Casey. Just show up there like a new girl who's Uncle might be moving to town and get them to trust you a bit," Douglas smiled.

"I'm twenty years old."

"You look fifteen," McAfee answered.

"And you look like a big ol' bear who's stolen way too many picnic baskets."

Douglas laughed. "Listen, it would really help us out. Record it on your phone, mention that your Uncle knows Jeremy's parents, maybe they say something."

"What if the cult children all turn on me right then and there?"

"We'll be right there nearby watching with binoculars," McAfee said. "This ain't my first rodeo. You'll be perfectly safe."

Casey was sitting on the sofa studying with her best friends,Emma and Tasha, who were enrolled in pre-law at

Georgia State. Douglas and McAfee had just returned from a long day in Jefferson, interviewing, studying and perhaps even provoking some of the locals.

"Are you guys sure she'll be safe?" Emma asked.

"Perfectly." Douglas replied. "You know I would never consider it otherwise."

"I don't want anything to happen to my peach."

"She won't leave our sight for one second."

"It would look good on my resume. A little Investigative work." Casey said.

"I think it will be a good experience for you as well. This is what we do, the family business," he winked.

"The whole story sounds so crazy," Tasha shook her head. "Are we really still dealing with this type of thing in the twenty-first century?"

"Sadly, yes," Douglas replied. And a whole lot more that sometimes stays hidden from the mainstream. We think this boy was actually driven to take his own life, not only by bullies his own age but grown people in town as well."

Casey had assisted with investigations before, several over the past year as a matter of fact, but never with direct involvement in the field. She was a terrific researcher with a great sense for finding supporting materials and tracking down long lost documents. But this was a whole other direction, a potentially risky one.

"I'm in. When are we doin' this?"

"Tomorrow's Friday. We think that means it will be extra busy in the evening at the Dairy Queen," McAfee answered. "You free?"

"Yeah, I still have a week till my papers are due. I can work on them over the weekend."

McAfee leaned forward in his seat. "So, you keep your phone on, someplace it won't be muffled, on the live line with Powell. We'll keep His muted so we hear you but they can't hear us."

"So I just start talking to people I've never met?"

"We're thinking some of the boys will approach you," Douglas smiled.

"Right, so I'm fresh meat."

"It's a small town. They'll take an interest. But yeah, no problem with talking to whoever you feel might be looking for a friend. You're just asking around about town and what they do for fun. Drop it into the conversation that you just heard about the boy who killed himself. See what shakes loose."

"I can't believe y'all have me going back to deal with High School assholes again."

"I'll tell you one thing," McAfee answered. "You've got a thick skin when it comes to that kind of crap. Just think about that small town boy without a friend in the world who obviously absorbed every hateful word they sent his way. There's nothing worse than an idiot with a big damn mouth."

"I never understood why people can't just live their own lives and leave everybody else alone," Casey shook her head. "I never will understand."

"They're just plain mean," Emma agreed. "And if someone dying doesn't change them then nothing's going to."

Casey walked the block from where Douglas and Lloyd waited in the car beside Smith's grocery store to the Dairy Queen. She looked to be the very picture of a Georgia girl, in cutoff denim shorts and Lynyrd Skynyrd t-shirt, not at all a stretch for her. She reached the busy parking lot and patio area at exactly five-thirty. There were maybe thirty people either waiting or sitting at the picnic tables enjoying their treats, most of them definitely High School age but a couple families as well. A few of the boys smiled at her and nodded as she approached the window to order. She pretended a shy smile in return.

"What can I get you sweetie?" The girl at the window asked.

"Hi, Can I get a double scoop of Strawberry in a sugar cone please?"

"Coming right up Darlin'."

As she waited she turned to survey the group. Just as the guys had expected she was the main attraction. She saw a few staring and they averted their eyes quickly when they saw she'd spotted them. A few of the boys were a bit bolder, looking her over like a sports car they'd like to drive. "Little Pervs," she mumbled. Back in the car Douglas and McAfee smiled.

The cashier brought her cone and Casey thanked her as she paid. It was warm, and she wrapped a napkin around the cone to catch the ice cream from dripping down onto her hand. There was no place to sit and so she very slowly walked back and forth a bit as she licked her cone. Four boys were seated at the table closest to her. One of them smiled at her. "Hey."

"Hey," she answered quietly, averting her eyes and looking shy.

"Come sit with us."

"Oh," she smiled. "I'm fine, thank you."

"Come on now. We won't bite."

She hesitated for just another moment. "Y'all sure you don't mind none?"

"Course not," he smiled again and elbowed the boy next to him to slide down.

Casey took a seat and offered a smile to the boys, clearly having their complete attention.

"So, this where y'all hang out usually?"

The boy across from her nodded. "Not a whole lot else going on. It's just a place to chill that's close for everybody. I'm Danny by the way."

"Casey."

"Hi Casey, That's Ronnie, Mike and Jessie."

Casey smiled politely to each of them. She turned to Jessie, the boy who'd invited her to join them. "So all of you go to Jefferson High?"

"Yup, Juniors. How about you? You're not from here or we'd know you."

"No, I live with my Uncle and he's thinking of moving us here from Atlanta."

"What the hell for? It sucks here."

"Well, I guess he thinks it'll be a better influence for me. Small town life and all."

"So, what d'you think so far?"

"It's quiet for sure."

"I'd be happy to show you around anytime."

The other boys grinned. Yeah, you're slick, Casey thought. "Maybe, sure."

Back in the car Douglas and McAfee listened to the exchange.

"She's a natural," McAfee smirked.

Douglas nodded. "That's my girl."

Casey laughed a little at corny jokes and boyish lines before pushing a bit.

"I heard about the boy that committed suicide. Did you know him?"

"Him," Mike spat, "More like her. Yeah, we knew it."

"It?"

"A little freak boy. The town bitch."

"Oh, did he do something to you?"

"He did something to us just by being here. Nobody wants that trash around them."

"What exactly did he do?"

"He was a freak. You know, a fag."

"He was gay?"

"Yeah, exactly. And he couldn't keep that shit to himself either, he had to spill it all over fuckin' town."

"He came out you mean?"

"Whatever."

"Kind of brave in a town like this. Don't you think?"

None of them answered. After a moment Danny got to his feet. "We gotta go. See you around I guess. Though Atlanta is probably best for you."

"How about that tour of town?" She asked as the others got up.

"You should stay in Atlanta."

The boys left her sitting alone and headed off on foot down the street.

"Something I said?" She mumbled to herself. "Bye assholes."

She glanced around and spotted a shy looking girl who seemed to be watching her. She was pretty, perhaps a bit nerdy looking, with red hair and wide rimmed glasses. She held a paperback book in her hands. Casey smiled her way and the girl smiled back. After a moment she got up from her seat and approached Casey.

"Hey, I'm Shelby. Shelby Lawson."

"Hi, Casey Malone. Please, sit with me."

"Thanks." Shelby wore a country sundress and sneakers and had a shy manner about her. A bookworm, Casey thought. My people. "I'm new around here, I guess you figured."

"That's why I wanted to say Hi. It sucks being the new kid."

"You've been there huh?"

"No, I wish. I've been stuck here all my life."

"It seems like a cute little town. The boys were a bit on the judgemental side I'd have to say."

"My brother Danny and his shadows. Not nice people."

"Oh, my bad. I didn't realize he was your brother."

"No need to apologize. We can't stand each other."

"You do seem a lot different. I asked about the boy who died and mentioned that he sounded brave and I guess that was it for me."

"Yeah, they'll hate you forever now. Join the club. But you're right, Jeremy was brave."

"Was he your friend?"

"Sorta. My Dad wouldn't let me hang out with him or anything. He's meaner than my brother."

"Gotcha."

"I wish I had though. After what happened I couldn't help but think if I'd been a better friend then maybe he wouldn't have done it."

"You were scared. I know what it's like."

"I feel like that's not an excuse. I should have stood up for him."

It was nearly seven by the time Casey climbed into the backseat. "You heard okay?"

"Perfectly," Douglas answered. "Pretty telling."

"At least we know that not everybody thinks the way the bullies do."

"Yeah," McAfee agreed, "but they're scared of the ones who do think that way."

"Well you can think whatever the hell you want, "Douglas said. "What you can't do is bully and harass a kid into hanging himself."

"I was thinking of Paulina the whole time. It's like the same story," Casey sighed.

"I bet you were. It had to be hard on you to do this. But it gives us insight. The bullies who drove your friend to suicide and these kids all operate the same way. Intimidation of the group in order to target one or a few without interference. What we need to do now is get some stories from some of the kids who are too afraid to speak up, like Shelby."

"Well," Casey replied, "you better be really careful not to expose anybody. I could tell Shelby is scared of her brother and his boys."

"You think she'll tell you more?" McAfee asked.

"We exchanged numbers. I don't think she's got too many friends here . So yeah, maybe so."

———————◆————————

Week Two

They'd agreed to meet up in the little town of Smith's Grove, just about in the middle of Atlanta and Jefferson. The town was a picture perfect throwback to old Georgia with narrow brick streets, quaint little shops, beautiful apple orchards and a gorgeous white gazebo right in the middle of the downtown. Since the weather was nice Casey and Shelby decided to have lunch, or as it were, Sunday brunch, at an outdoor cafe. Shelby had seemed a bit anxious at first until Casey started talking about books and that they should check out the little used bookstore down the street.

"I saw you reading at the Dairy Queen the other night. What're you into?" Casey asked.

"A little of everything," Shelby smiled. "I like fantasy the best but I can get into a little Sci-fi and sometimes even some of the Christian teen novels."

"Christain huh?" Casey scrunched up her nose.

Shelby laughed. "I know, I know. Some of it's a little corny. I just like a nice clean story sometimes you know?"

"Okay, so, sometimes I still read Nancy Drew."

Shelby grinned widely. "Is that so?"

"I just love that bitch. She's cool as hell. Don't tell anybody."

"Hey, I'm with you. A good clean story."

"Exactly."

They finished their biscuits and gravy and headed out on foot to take a look around. Casey suggested they head down to the bookshop. "I'm surprised so many places are open."

"Yeah, they have a lot of weekend visitors so they probably need to."

"I saw a couple Bed and Breakfasts on my way in."

"Yeah and there's some cottage rentals too."

"Cute place."

"It really is."

They were almost to the shop when Shelby suddenly blurted out, "I know who you are."

Casey stopped walking and grinned. "I told you who I am. I'm Casey Malone."

"Yes, but you're the Casey Malone."

Casey nodded. "I suppose I am. I? Guess you're okay with that or you wouldn't be here."

"I was curious. Plus you seemed really nice the other day, and you still do. So, you're not a High School student anymore are you?"

"I was until very recently. I completed an accelerated program to get it wrapped up."

"So why are you here?"

"Well today I'm here cause I really wanted to chill with you. But Friday I was there to try and find out a little about Jeremy."

"You're helping that reporter aren't you?"

"Journalist. He hates being called a reporter."

"Why's he interested in Jeremy?"

"Because Jeremy's folks asked him to be. They believe their son did what he did because people treated him so badly."

"Oh my God, is my brother in trouble?"

"I don't know. Did he kill Jeremy?

"No, of course not."

"Did he bully him until he decided to kill himself?"

"I...."

"You don't have to answer that. He's your brother. But I would like to know about some of the things Jeremy went through in School."

They went inside the book shop and spent the next hour rummaging through discount bins and a clearance rack. Casey was pleased to see that they had a music section in the back and she picked out a vinyl album by John Lee Hooker for Douglas. He enjoyed having some Blues playing softly in the background while he did his writing at home.

"Hey," Casey grabbed a paperback from the shelf and held it up. "Assassin's apprentice."

"No way," Shelby came and looked it over. "It's a first edition. In good shape too."

"You should grab it."

"I think I will, Thanks.

They paid for their selections and made their way slowly toward the gazebo to sit for a little while.

"So," Casey said. "Apple fritters huh?"

"Oh my god Casey, they're so good. You gotta try some."

"I'm more of a peach cobbler girl."

"You just wait. I bet you change your mind."

"How does a town surrounded by cotton get the tag of Apple fritter capital of the world anyway?"

"Baking contests," Shelby smiled. "Jefferson is all about growing cotton and baking pies and fritters. Our town's the County seat but the rest of the area, like here in Smith's Grove, is all Apple Orchards. So people get pretty wound up about winning ribbons at the fair."

"Got ya. So people practice on their families and friends all year long to win the baking contests each year."

"Yup. There's the County fair, Halloween bash, Christmas bake-off, Harvest celebration, Founder's day, fourth of July...."

"Yikes, that's a lot of baking."

"I love it. I'll bake some for you myself."

"I'll be happy to eat whatever you bake my friend."

Shelby smiled but seemed to lower her head just a little. Casey knew the look all too well.

"I don't have many friends now," she said. "A few real good ones but I had a hard time since I was a kid as far as that goes."

Shelby met her gaze. "I call a couple people my friends, and they call me theirs, but we're not."

"Why?"

40

"I just don't like the way they act sometimes. Or the things they say. They've kinda got a mean streak you know?"

"Yeah. Like your brother and the other boys I met."

"Right," she nodded. "People seem set in their ways here and if you don't agree with them you're pretty much out in the cold."

"Will you tell me about Jeremy a little bit. Give me some idea of the stuff he was dealing with."

"People can't hear I said anything about it."

"They won't, I promise."

"Okay," Shelby sighed. "Well, there was one day everybody knows about. It was pretty bad. I mean, really, really bad."

School had just started back and Shelby was as nervous as anyone else to be in High School. At the same time she was one year closer to getting into a decent college and eventually getting out of Jefferson for good. It wasn't that things were horrible for her, that wouldn't be at all fair to say. She was well taken care of and lived in a beautiful house with food always available and she never doubted that her parents loved her. That very morning her Dad had knocked on her bedroom door and asked to speak with her for a moment. He was on his way to open the Barber shop but wanted to give her something first. He hung the most beautiful gold chain around her neck with a sweet little heart charm. "I'm really proud of you," he'd said. "You're going to set the world on fire."

The smile was plastered on her face for the entire bus ride into school and even through the somewhat scary process of orientation and getting her bearings. At her Dad's insistence Danny had offered to take her with him in his car but she'd decided that a certain degree of separation would be best. He was a Junior this year, and a major dumbass, and she didn't want to be labeled by association. He and the other jocks were well known all over town for messing with people and she was just the opposite. She enjoyed helping others and volunteering and couldn't for the life of her understand why the boys acted that way. Like her Dad. She loved him, but it was true. He could be mean as a rattler and some of the things that came out of his mouth were shameful.

She had been searching through the East hallway for her Earth Science classroom and was lucky enough to come across a girl's room. Thank goodness cause her Mama had insisted on her eating breakfast this morning and the tall glass of orange juice was catching up. Peeing her pants in class her first day of school did not sound like a fun plan at all. The first bell rang as she washed her hands. The bells rang twice she'd learned in orientation, One with a minute and a half warning and the second to signal the start of class. Everybody was moving quickly into their classrooms when she walked back into the hallway and she started toward the open door of her own class and the smiling face of whom she presumed was Mrs. Keller. A few of the older kids had said Mrs. Keller was their favorite and went easy on everybody. Even Danny who hardly ever did his homework.

She was just passing the boy's bathroom when she thought she heard the sound of someone crying. Her immediate thought was that somebody was really scared to be starting High School and probably had psyched themselves up into a full on panic attack. But as she listened the crying sounded like more than that, pained. She saw Mrs. Keller step inside the classroom and knew she only had maybe thirty seconds before she'd officially be late for her very first class. She put her ear up to the bathroom door and listened to the sobbing. She tapped a couple times and when nobody answered she cracked the door open just a few inches.

"Hello."

The crying continued but no one responded.

She pushed the door open a few more inches. "Hello in there. Are you okay?"

Still no answer.

"Hey, It's Shelby Lawson. Do I know you? Do you need some help?"

The hallway was nearly clear and Mrs. Keller came to the doorway for one last look before she got down to business. Shelby caught her attention and waved her over. Mrs. Keller came to stand beside her.

"I think somebody's upset Ma'am."

Mrs. Keller pushed open the door all the way and called in. "Young man, are you alright?"

There was still no response but the sound of sobbing continued.

Mrs. Keller entered the bathroom with Shelby on her heels and walked to the stall where the sobbing was coming from. She tapped her knuckles a couple times on the stall door. "Hey, are you okay in there? This is Mrs. Keller. Do you need help?"

When nobody answered she pushed on the stall door and found it unlatched. A boy sat crouched between the toilet and partition, lip bloodied and face bruised. His pants were undone and he was clutching them to himself in terror.

"Go right now to the office and tell them we need help," She said to Shelby.

Shelby was clearly upset as she recounted the story.

"When they got him to his feet there was blood soaked through the back of his pants Casey."

"Oh my god. They raped him?"

44

"I don't know. They kept it all very quiet and told me not to say a word for his protection and privacy."

"It was Jeremy."

"Yes."

"Jesus."

"Yeah."

"You two were already friends at that point?"

"Kinda. We would talk here and there but he pretty much always kept to himself."

"So nothing ever came of it that you know of? I mean. That's pretty damn major to happen right in school."

"I heard rumors circulating around about Jeremy but nothing about any attack."

"Rumors like what?"

"Like he would drive out to the highway at night and have sex with truckers at the rest stop for money."

"Original."

"Yeah. Also that he made gay porn videos and sold them online."

"Who was saying this stuff?"

"My brother and the other boys. I heard my Dad and the other men saying some pretty nasty stuff at his shop too."

Casey glanced around the town center. Smith's Grove really was a pretty little place. As peaceful as it was it was not surprising that it welcomed so many weekend visitors. People were browsing the little shops and heading out to u-pick-it events at the local orchards. It was definitely a date weekend kind of destination but there were families as well. It all made her wonder if the same ugliness lurked beneath the surface that seemed to plague Jefferson.

"When was the last time you actually talked with Jeremy?"

Shelby looked away sadly. "Just two days before he...you know."

"Was that in school?"

"No. I was riding my bike into town to pick up some sugar from Smith's for my Mama. I saw Jeremy come out of the church so I stopped to say hi."

"How did he seem to you?"

"Sad. More than that. More than sad."

"Suicidal."

"I keep thinking I could have done something. I should have done something."

"It's not like you've had a lot of experience dealing with people in a rough emotional state Shelby. What did he say?"

"I asked if he was going to be performing with the school orchestra at the fall festival. Mama and I were already signed up for the bake-off."

"What'd he say?"

"He said no because….umm."

"Because why?"

"You can't say anything Casey."

"I won't mention your name to anybody."

"He said his Dad told him that stuff's for fags and he was embarrassing him."

Douglas, McAfee, and Sammy, the Chief Editor of the Atlanta Daily, were already sipping their coffee in Sammy's office when Casey arrived at eleven o'clock on Monday morning. As she made her way through the reporter's bullpen, John Fitzpatrick winked at her. "When are we going on that date Casey?"

"The sooner you get to sleep the sooner your dream will come true John," she winked back. The other journalists laughed as John pretended to doze off at his desk.

"Nice of you to join us Malone," Sammy said without looking up from her papers.

"You do know I'm a full time student right Sammy?"

"Excuses. So let's go. Where are we at with this thing?"

"Well, from what Casey told us we may have an unreported hate crime," McAfee answered.

Douglas nodded. "And Jeremy's Dad wasn't exactly as forthcoming as we'd thought. We need to dig a bit deeper into that for sure."

"Probably why they haven't retained a lawyer yet," Sammy noted. "If the word got out that the Dad was gay shaming the kid himself that would hurt any legal case for sure. Maybe they think if you guys exert pressure on the School Board that they'll make some backroom settlement offer."

Casey took a bite out of one of the donuts on Sammy's desk and made a face. "This shit's stale."

"Focus Malone," Sammy handed her a napkin to spit it out. "You think we can get any more from the girl?"

"I'm sure she knows more. But she's a little apprehensive of course."

"Maybe you can connect with some of the other students. Get a feel for the place as a whole."

"Well, if the boys I met are any indication..."

"Fuck the boys. High school boys are always assholes, you know that. Reach out to more of the girls. Try to corroborate this whole idea of an entire town of bigots.

"I need some money," Casey answered between sips of coffee.

"Money for what?"

"Uh, a decent donut for one thing boss. Not to mention Dairy Queen, secret lunches, gas, books."

"Books my ass. Feed your own addiction."

"Fine. But the rest is straight up legit."

Douglas smirked. "Undercover work is costly, boss lady."

"Fine, whatever. One hundred bucks from petty cash. Make it last Malone, this ain't CNN."

"Well, it's been fun kids," Casey said, " but I'd rather not flunk outta college my first year so I'm gonna bounce."

"Okay Casey. Lloyd and I are gonna head back to Jefferson and see if we can get a word with the Pastor of the church Jeremy attended with his folks. Maybe get an off the record on the family dynamic."

"Alright cool. Bring home pizza. And don't forget my hundred bucks. And I have receipts for yesterday too."

"How does she not give you a damn headache?" McAfee mumbled.

"I got you," Douglas laughed. "Go write those papers."

In the early afternoon Jefferson reminded Douglas of some of the towns you'd see on black and white televisions programs from the sixties. There was very little traffic, sometimes none at all, with everyone at work or school or, he presumed, home baking apple fritters. It was also the time of year when lots of the cotton crop was being harvested. Depending upon weather that could run from the fall straight through till January. The town was decorated with pumpkin displays, scarecrows, and a huge banner across Main street announcing the annual harvest festival.

"Looks like a safe place to trick or treat," he said.

"If you're not a gay kid," McAfee grunted.

Douglas nodded. The truth of it was really disturbing. McAfee was not one to mince words. But yeah, the reality was this was not a gay-bashing outside a bar or a refusal to bake a cake for a customer you disliked. All of that was bad enough. But this was a child. How could everyone not be up in arms over this?

They pulled into the gravel parking lot of the United Christian Church of Jefferson. What exactly were they united about? He wondered. The place looked to be over one hundred years old. Whitewashed wood siding, a metal roof that was clearly not original to the building, wide front steps with dark wood railings. The stained glass was exquisite. Just beyond the grassy rear of the building was the church cemetery which appeared to be full up.

"Looks nice enough," he commented.

"This shit pisses me off."

"What's that?"

"The hypocrisy."

"Yeah, I know."

"I mean, look at this little house on the prairie bullshit. Like they didn't just contribute to a young boy deciding to kill himself."

"I know."

"Assholes."

"Yeah."

They sat for a moment just looking around the grounds a bit.

"Peaceful though," McAfee added grudgingly.

"You good? If you're not feeling this?"

"I'm fine. I've been dealing with lying scumbags all my life."

"Just don't punch the preacher. Please."

"Yeah. Let's get it over with."

The front door was locked and no one answered their knocking. There were a couple of cars parked near the back door so they walked back that way. A small brass sign beside the door said Church office. There was no bell so they made their way inside to a waiting area with an elderly woman at the desk waiting to greet them. "Good day Ma'am," Douglas smiled.

She smiled curtly. "Good day."

"Is the Pastor available please?"

"Do you have an appointment?"

"Why is he overrun with visitors?" McAfee grumbled.

Douglas took out his I.D. "I'm Douglas Powel and this is Detective McAfee. We'd just like a few moments of his time if it's not too much trouble."

She looked at them disapprovingly before instructing them to take a seat for a moment. Douglas gave McAfee a slight nudge with his elbow. "Curb it Lloyd."

"Whatever."

After a moment the lady returned and nodded to them. "Pastor Reynolds will see you now."

She ushered them back into the Pastor's office, a rather small wood panelled space with an ancient looking carpet and lots of over-packed bookcases. The Pastor pulled his large frame up from behind his desk and smiled warmly. "Gentlemen, please come in and grab a seat."

He reached over to shake each of their hands before plopping himself back down again. "So, what can I do for the big city press and the police? Is that right?"

"Retired," McAfee replied. "I'm a Private Investigator now working as a consultant for the Daily."

"I see. Well, how can I help?"

"We're looking into the death of Jeremy Timmons," McAfee answered. "Wondering what you might be able to tell us about him and his family."

The Pastor shook his head. "Terrible. That poor boy was really loved. Sometimes mental health issues just seem to creep up without any red flags."

"Did he ever come to you? Discuss any problems he may be having?"

"No, not ever. He always seemed to be such a well adjusted young man."

"We know he was here a couple of days before he passed. Can you tell us what that visit was for?"

"Well, I do know sometimes he would come in just to sit in the sanctuary. To pray I assume. Lots of our congregants do the same."

"He never reached out to you with any concerns? Tell you about any personal problems or troubles at home?"

"No," the Pastor shook his head. "Like I said, he was always quiet, well mannered, polite."

"Were you aware that Jeremy was gay?"

"I'd heard a rumor or two. Not that I would ever encourage rumors of course. I never paid it much mind,"

"But he never intimated any personal struggles to you? Discussed any problems at home or anything?"

"No, I'm sorry but nothing."

Douglas looked over the Pastor's diploma's on the wall as McAfee asked his questions. He'd graduated from Georgia State before going on to earn a Master of Divinity and then a Doctorate from Southern Theological Seminary.

"You're an educated man," Douglas smiled.

The Pastor returned his smile. "Well, you must be prepared to defend the faith. Apologetics require knowledge."

"Tell us about Ted Lawson."

The Pastor's smile faded away. "Ted? He's uh, well, he's one of our Deacons here at the church."

Douglas was shocked. "He's a what?"

"A Deacon, yes. Going on twenty years now I think."

"I'm gonna hop on out and catch some air now," McAfee nodded to the Pastor and headed out the door.

"Is he okay?"

"He's fine, Pastor. Long car ride. So tell me, Ted's a Deacon? I'm sorry but I don't see it."

Pastor Reynolds smiled again. "Right. Well, he's a good leader for the youth. The boys really look up to him."

"Do they now?"

"A real man of God."

"Is that so?"

"Indeed."

"Pastor, how many congregants do y'all have?"

"Seventy very fine families, Mister Powell. About two hundred sixty folks in all."

"Wow. That's quite a job for you."

"I love what I do but yes, it's busy. That's why the Deacon's are essential."

"So Ted's a youth pastor?"

"Unofficially, sure. For the boys. Miss Rose works with the girls. She's another fine lady who's been involved for years."

"Instilling the young folk with values."

"Of course."

Douglas sat for a second, wondering if the Pastor was clueless or covering up.

He decided to just tear off the tape. "Is Ted teaching them to be bigots?"

"I beg your pardon?"

"Bigots. Racists, homophobes, misogynists, stop me when I hit one that's not true."

The Pastor seemed a bit shaken now. "I'm not sure what you're implying, Mister Powell, but none of that is true."

"So Ted doesn't teach the boys of this church and this town to hate kids who are different."

"Certainly not."

"Are you sure?"

The Pastor went to say something but then stopped. Douglas got to his feet.

"Thank you for your time Pastor. When you see Ted please tell him we said hello."

McAfee was leaning against the car reading something on his cellphone when Douglas came out.

"Well, that was...enlightening."

McAfee shook his head. "No wonder they listen to him, he's a Deacon."

"They have a right to teach whatever they want as far as lifestyle choices are concerned. All I care about is whether they went so far as to emotionally torture this boy to death."

"So, who are we after here? The original assignment was to check into any wrongdoing by the School Board."

"I think there's a whole lot more than that to look into here. I'm worried about the whole sorta environment of intolerance they seem to have going on."

"I'll tell you who we need to talk to," McAfee agreed. "Jeremy's twin sister, Emily."

"Funny, I've been thinking the same thing. We'd have to tread very lightly. She just lost her twin only a month ago."

"Malone's gotta do it."

"How do we even get them to meet up. We haven't seen Emily out and about with any of the other kids."

"Maybe Shelby Lawson knows her. Could be they're friends."

"Alright, let's get outta here."

"Stop at that little bakery down the road. I want some of them fritters."

"Your wife's gonna kill me."

"She'll never know."

Casey sat in the college library typing on her laptop and occasionally stopping to scan through one or more of the open books that surrounded her on the table. She liked her Sociology Professor but boy could the guy dish out the work. You wanna know about people, she thought to herself, most of them suck ass. Class dismissed.

You had to do what you had to do if you wanted to earn a degree and make a decent living. Sociology, Philosophy, Art history, whatever it was, you just drove your way through it. It was beneficial as far as developing research skills and polishing her writing so it wasn't a total waste of time. But gosh could it be boring.

She was immersed in a particularly fact-heavy paragraph when a shadow blocked just a bit of the light that had been streaming through the window onto her keyboard. She looked up to a young guy standing on the other side of her table flashing his best James Dean smile at her. He was good looking, she'd give him that much, with dark hair and sincere eyes. He raised his chin just slightly, "Hey there, anyone sitting here?"

She glanced around at the six or seven open tables then back to him. "I suppose not if there's something particularly inviting to you about this table."

"Oh yeah, there definitely is."

Cheesy, she thought as he pulled out a chair opposite her and took a seat. "I'm Jerry," he said.

Casey went back to her typing.

"And you are?"

"Busy."

Jerry laughed a little as he opened his book. "Got it. Nice to meet you, Busy."

Casey felt her phone vibrate in her back pocket and pulled it out to check her text. It was Douglas. "Veal Parm tonight? I'll pick it up from Tony's."

She texted him back, "That sounds awesome."

She tried to get back to her work but felt Jerry watching her.

"Your boyfriend checking up on you?" he asked.

She ignored him.

"Hope he's not the jealous type."

She looked up and met his goofy gaze. "He has nothing to be jealous of 'cause I have no idea who you are."

"Well I was trying to get your number."

"By annoying me?"

"Whatever works."

Casey leaned back in her seat and looked closer at Jerry. He was actually pretty cute, annoying as all hell but cute. He was wearing jeans and a white collared shirt and was clean cut and shaven. She guessed he was about six foot tall.

"What are you pretending to study over there?" she asked.

"Economics."

"Why economics?"

"I'm planning on eventually working in the financial field."

"Pyramid schemes and such?"

"Don't knock it till you tried it, Busy."

She couldn't help herself from smiling just a bit. It widened his smile.

"My name's Casey."

"I like it."

"I'm so glad."

"So what do you like to do when you're not studying Miss Casey?"

"The usual. Assist with investigations into political corruption, hate crimes, scandals, stuff like that."

"Wow. What are you like Nancy Drew or something?"

"I wish. I love that bitch."

"Who doesn't?"

Casey decided she liked him. So far at least. They could all be quite charming at first but monsters never showed their true face until it was too late and you were already caught in their snare. She checked her watch and began to close up her books and pack her computer. She tore a scrap of paper out of her notebook and jotted down her number. As she got to her feet she slid it across the table to him. "Don't make me regret this Jerry."

"Hammond."

"Pardon?"

He got to his feet and held out his hand. "Jerry Hammond."

"Casey Malone," she nodded as she shook it.

"Can I call you tonight?"

"Tomorrow. Tonight I'm having dinner with the most important man in my life."

"Your Dad I hope?"

"Bye Jerry," she grinned as she walked away.

The veal parm was so good it should be illegal. It was a beautiful evening outside, seventy and clear with a slight breeze. Casey and Douglas had decided to eat their dinner out on the balcony and were now enjoying a couple slices of cheesecake and some sweet tea.

"So y'all think the Pastor is one of them? She asked.

"No, I don't think so. I think he's just clueless. People don't usually run to their Pastor to talk about how hateful they are."

"Unless they're confessing."

"Right, and these guys don't believe for one second that they're in the wrong."

Casey set her plate down. "I met a guy today."

"Oh yeah? Where?"

"A little while ago in the library. He's a finance major, seems pretty nice I guess."

"That's great Casey. Did you make any plans to talk further?"

"He asked for my number, I gave it to him. So we'll see."

"Well I think that's great. If it's just a new friend that's great too."

"You know I don't trust easily."

"Yeah, you and me both, kid. A hazard of this business. Just go real slow and see what shakes out. And get his date of birth so Lloyd can run him through the system."

Casey laughed. "I almost asked for it today."

"That's my girl."

"So, we were thinking."

"Oh no."

"Nothing bad I promise. We're thinking that we need to try to talk with Emily Timmons, Jeremy's twin sister, and maybe get the inside scoop on their homelife and perhaps if he intimated any stories from school to her."

"Yeah. Especially about the attack in the bathroom."

"She's his twin so you never know. They tend to be closer than other siblings."

"So how do we do it?"

"We thought maybe Shelby and her are friends? Maybe she can arrange a girls day out or something?"

"Hmm. Shelby never mentioned Emily but that doesn't mean anything. I can always ask."

They sat for a moment listening to the John Lee Hooker album that Casey had brought home from Smith's Grove. Douglas reached over and gave Casey's hand a squeeze. She smiled at him. "What?"

"Nothing."

"Thanks for dinner. I think I gained five pounds."

"Gosh, me too."

"It's so nice out tonight."

"It's beautiful."

"Halloween's coming up."

"I know you love it."

"You have to dress up with me this year."

"Maybe Casanova will want to take you to a party."

"Jerry," she smirked.

"I'm jealous."

"So make the date with me now before he gets the chance. You and me, Halloween night in costumes at the downtown street party."

Douglas shook his head and grinned. "Fine. I can't believe you've got me doing this."

"You can't back out neither."

"Never on you."

Week Three

Casey moved quickly down the hall and headed for the exit. The Language Arts building was the largest on campus and if you were a fitness buff keeping track of your steps you could log a ton just navigating the hallways. Her English Lit class had just ended and it was nearly eleven. She'd have a few hours to work on her paper before heading out to meet up with Shelby and Emily in Smith's Grove, away from prying eyes and even worse, ears. It turned out that Shelby and Emily were friends, which might work out well as far as information gathering went. If Shelby was cooperating and trying to help then of course Emily would want to. Jeremy was her brother after all.

It bothered Casey that Emily's Dad may have been the one pushing the most hurtful buttons though. A bunch of stupid kids talking smack was one thing but your own Dad? She couldn't help but flash back to her own Daddy, calling her useless, retarded, using her like a toy then throwing her aside like trash. She found herself wondering now and then where her parents were. Was her Mama okay? Was she living on the street or in some shelter maybe? All that time that Casey had sat there in prison and not even a note from her. Actions speak louder than words, she thought. Her Mama had chance after chance to make things right. She'd never really talked to anyone about the day that Mama found out about what Casey's Daddy had been up to.

It was months before she'd even met Jimmy Ward. She was still fourteen, working very limited hours at the convenience store and spending all her spare time reading and studying. The weather was actually quite pretty that day, right about seventy-five degrees and bright sunshine. She passed by Mrs. Tenshaw's house as she made her way home and could smell the freshly baked pie through the open window. The smell of fresh baked treats had always made her smile. Her mind would take her off to somewhere homey and secure. She wondered what it must be like to live in a house like that with a Mama who cooked and baked and a Daddy who'd come home and play with the kids and ask them all about their day. She bet that Mr. and Mrs. Tenshaw probably tucked their kids in at night and gave them a kiss on the forehead.

When she reached her house it looked quiet, as it normally would this time of the day. Her Daddy's car was there but it had been all week since the muffler had gone and was so loud the cops had warned Daddy that if they caught him driving it one more time he'd get a fat ticket.

One of his work buddies had been picking him up each day in exchange for a little gas money. Mama's care was gone too cause she'd be out at the bar with her girlfriends and would usually stay there till after dark.

Casey made her way inside and was doubly relieved when nobody appeared in the kitchen or living room. She grabbed the pitcher of lemonade from the fridge and poured herself half a glass and brought it with her back to her room to get started on homework. She turned her radio on real low to one of the Atlanta Country stations and stretched out on her belly across the bed with her books. She'd been halfway through reading the chapter her Social Studies teacher had assigned when she felt someone watching her. She looked up quickly to see her Daddy in the doorway, leaning against the frame and grinning his evil grin. She could just make out the whiff of alcohol even from across the room. She sat up on the bet and kept her eyes lowered.

"Hi Daddy."

"Don't get up on my account sweet girl. Daddy just came in to say hello and see how his baby is doin' today."

"I'm fine Daddy. How are you?"

He entered the room and closed the door behind him, the fear welling up inside of her to the point she could hardly breathe. He sauntered over toward her, barely able to keep on his feet. There was no escape, no way she'd be able to fight him off or make it past him to the door. He came to stand right in front of her and began to stroke her hair. He lifted her chin up with his index finger and she looked into his eyes. She knew the look all too well. Something horrible was about to happen to her.

"Look at those pretty lips," he whispered.

He began to unbutton his shirt when the bedroom door suddenly burst open and her Mama came in.

"You piece of goddamn shit!"

She began to smack Casey's Daddy over and over again, punching him in the head and screaming profanities at him. He shoved her off and made his way out of the room, leaving her Mama panting from the exertion. After a moment she turned to Casey. "Put some decent clothes on. You look like a little goddamn whore!"

Casey suddenly felt a hand on her shoulder and she nearly jumped out of her skin. She wheeled around to see Jerry's startled face. He took a few quick steps back.

"I'm so sorry Casey, I didn't mean to scare you."

She looked around the busy hallway for a moment, snapping back into the present and clearing her mind. "It's cool Jerry. My bad. I was just lost in my own little world for a minute. Sorry about that."

"No, don't apologize. I snuck up on you. Sure you're okay?"

"Yeah, I'm fine. Class stress, you know."

"Yeah, I feel you. I just spotted you and thought maybe we could grab an early lunch if you're free?"

Casey smiled a little. "Yeah, why not."

The School's cafeteria was large but always clean and the food, although far from great, was immensely better than the food in prison. Casey had learned many lessons on the inside, one of which was to be grateful for the little things including being able to eat anywhere as a free woman. There were many people in similar situations to her own who would never be able to eat where they wanted or go for a walk whenever they pleased. There hadn't been many nights since she'd been out that she hadn't gone outside on the condo balcony to soak in the splendor of the stars, if only for a few moments. She was so immensely grateful for Douglas that sometimes just thinking about it made her cry. Crying itself was another thing you'd be ill advised to let people see in prison. Showing that kind of vulnerability could get you hurt or worse.

She sat lost in her thoughts for a moment, looking at the burger and fries on her tray and thinking about visitation days and microwave cheeseburgers with Douglas. He had never once complained about the food or the drive or the fact that he'd spent every single Sunday for seventy-six weeks visiting that awful place just to spend time with her.

She had never had anybody care about her that much and she would be grateful to him for the rest of her life for giving her back her dreams.

"Penny for your thoughts," Jerry smiled.

Casey looked up. "I'm so sorry Jerry."

"Looks like you're maybe having a bad day?"

She smiled. "Not for a very long time actually."

"Well, that's good to hear. I spend a lot of time stressed out."

"Oh I get stressed," she answered as she ate a fry. But anything close to a bad day? Nope. I've learned the difference."

"So you're one of those zen kinda people. Always calm in the storm."

She looked around for a second to see if anyone was within earshot, then back to him. "Listen, I really need to tell you something before we become friends."

"I thought we were already becoming friends."

"You know what I mean."

Jerry reached across the table and took her hand. "I know who you are Casey Malone. I know what you went through and that it was wrong and that you deserve to be happy now and enjoy your life."

Casey was a bit stunned, then guarded. "Did you know who I was when you approached me in the library? When you acted like you didn't know my name?"

"No, I didn't. I swear. I asked around a little and everybody said that you were nice and polite and studious...and reserved. That said you kept your head in your books and kept to yourself."

"And my story?"

"That you were a victim. A couple of them used the word brave. I agree by the way."

Casey went back to moving her fries around a bit on her plate.

"I'd like to call you tonight Casey, if that's still okay?"

She looked into his eyes a moment, looking for truth, for signs of any deception. It was built into her nature now and there was no trying to fight it.

"I'm going to need something from you Jerry."

"Anything. You want me to keep what we talked about confidential of course, I promise I will."

"No. I need you to write down your full name and date of birth. And don't forget to put your middle initial."

She'd managed a little bit of work in the library before it was time to head up to meet Shelby and Emily. They'd agreed on four o'clock at the gazebo which gave her just about an hour. Once she cleared the local traffic around the college it would be pretty smooth sailing on the way to Smith's Grove. As she drove she thought about Jerry. She hadn't even thought about being with another guy since getting out of prison and was surprised that she was even considering it. For the first time in her life she was actually happy with the way things were, content. There were no longer any fears or worries or nightmares, just true comfort from feeling loved and wanted and hopeful. If Douglas had never come to visit her, if he had passed on the assignment or been busy with another story...well then things would have gone much differently for Casey.

She arrived in Smith's Grove a little bit before four, pulling up in front of the gazebo and spotting Shelby and Emily already waiting for her. She climbed out and hit the lock button on her key fob, not that you needed it in this area. She doubted that there were many crimes at all much less vehicle thefts. Shelby waved and Casey walked across the manicured grass to them. "Y'all been waiting long?"

"Just got here girl," Shelby smiled. "Casey, this is Emily Timmons."

Casey reached out her hand and Emily took it. "Casey, nice to meet you Emily."

"You too. My parents told me some people were looking into my brother's death."

"We are. Can we sit for a few minutes?"

The girls took seats on the gazebo benches. "Your parents asked the Atlanta Daily to look into the factors leading to Jeremy's death. In particular the school doing nothing to stop the bullying he suffered."

Emily closed her eyes for a second then nodded to Casey. "It was pretty horrible for him."

"Did you witness a lot of it yourself?"

"Yes, and I didn't do enough to stop it either."

Emily wiped tears from her face and Casey gave her a moment. "Can you tell me about some of it, Emily?"

"My brother was always different from most of the other boys. He wasn't interested in playing baseball or other sports and he didn't like video games and all that stuff. He always wanted to tag along with me and my friends which was fine when we were little but it started to bother some of the other girls as we got older. You know how girls like to talk about stuff and they didn't feel comfortable with him around. When we got to Junior High he decided to come out as gay and told a few people. It seemed to spread to everyone in town within a few hours."

"I'm guessing Jefferson is not exactly gay friendly. How did people react?"

"Just like you'd expect. You grew up in a small town in Georgia so you know how it is."

"So, who was the first to mess with him?"

Emily glanced toward Shelby then quickly away.

"It's alright Emily," Shelby said. "You can tell her."

Emily looked concerned for Shelby's feelings. "The first was Shelby's brother, Danny, and all of his friends that he hangs out with."

"I met a bunch of them at the DQ."

"That's where they all hang out."

Casey could see the pain in Emily's eyes and though she didn't want to cause her any more, she still needed to get the facts.

"Can you tell me more about what happened?"

Emily took a deep breath and began to tell her story.

"It was our first day of school and I was kinda excited to finally be in High School and Jeremy didn't seem all that nervous either. I think maybe he was hoping since we were all a little older that some of the bullying and nonsense would be over with. But he was wrong, things only got worse for him."

Emily and Jeremy always got dropped off for school by their Mom. At that time of the morning, as early as it was, their Dad had already been out working the farm for several hours. None of the school busses ran that far out and their Mom never seemed to mind anyway. She'd just run some of her errands and do some visiting sometimes with folks in town that she did mending for in her spare time. She even made the prettiest dresses for Emily and some of her friends and seemed to get a lot of joy from doing it. But what she seemed to love the most was the quiet time in the car on the way to and from school when she could talk with her children and find out everything that was going on with them. Emily always talked the most, about classes and teachers, boys and the teen dramas of her friends. Jeremy was more reserved, answering politely when his Mama would ask a question but rarely interested in driving the conversation the way his sister did. He never seemed happy, but never quite sad either. He seemed to be going through the motions, doing what was expected, cooperating.

It was a pretty day, though already too hot at seven in the morning. Their Mama talked about how she'd lived in Georgia all her life and would never get used to the Summer heat. In Georgia, like most of the South, school returned in mid-August, and their Dad had always said that the air conditioning bills for the schools was why everyone's property taxes were so damn high. Emily never replied, even though she'd always figured it must be more on account of all the cops in town who weren't needed and didn't do crap. Chief Willie Charles was so damn fat he couldn't run if a bear was chasin' him. The others spent more time checking out the young girls with their creepy stares then doing any kind of police work. Truth was, since there was a County Sheriff's office there was really no need at all for a police department in Jefferson. But since Mayor Deen and the whole town council were best friends with Chief Willie, that was never gonna change.

When they pulled up in front of the school Emily leaned over to kiss her Mama on the cheek and Jeremy leaned over the seat from the back to do the same.

"Y'all do good and make me proud," she said as they jumped out. They walked together toward the door until Emily spotted a couple of her friends. "Alright, I'll see you later on Jeremy."

Jeremy nodded and watched his sister run to join her friends as he headed on toward the front doors. He knew that they didn't want him around anymore and it didn't feel good. These days it seemed like nobody wanted him around. Emily turned to watch as he went through the door with his head down low. She felt a twinge of guilt, hating to see her twin in pain, but what was she to do? At their age he just couldn't tag around with her everywhere she went anymore. When she'd told him that she thought for a moment that he might cry but he kept his composure. He'd just nodded and went out into the yard with his sketch pad. Then she cried.

There hadn't been any formal freshman orientation, just some seniors at a folding table who would look up your name in their folders and hand you a schedule and crude building map. A few school organizations were also on hand to pass out fliers and encourage participation in their varied activities. The more kids that signed up for a club the more budget money would be allocated to them. Emily was happy to spot her brother at the arts table, talking with a few of the other kids. She hoped that he would sign up for the school choir also because she knew how much he enjoyed singing. Maybe he'd make some good friends and this year wouldn't be as hard on him as she thought it might be. Those hopes were crushed quickly.

She'd only been in her first class for fifteen minutes when a lady from the office came on the speaker to request her immediate presence. Her teacher, Mister Klein, seemed as surprised as her that she'd be summoned so soon on her first day and she felt herself flush just a bit. She nodded for her to go ahead and handed her a new text book as she headed out the door. She thought maybe they had made a mistake with her class schedule and just needed to give her the correct one. Hopefully she'd be back in class within a few minutes so nobody would think she was already in trouble.

The lady behind the counter looked shaken as she escorted Emily across the hall to the nurses office. She was ushered into the small waiting area and introduced to the Principal Miss Marsh. Miss Marsh took her by the hand and invited her to sit. Emily could tell that the woman was normally in stern mode, with the look of a drill instructor and a crisp, navy blue business suit.

"Emily, your brother's been involved in an incident."

"Oh my God! Is he okay?"

"Well...we aren't quite sure yet. He's been hurt but he isn't answering any of our questions. We thought perhaps if you talked with him?"

"But I just saw him like twenty minutes ago and he was fine."

"Apparently something happened before the start of class."

"Is he hurt bad?"

"He's inside with Mrs. Turnboldt. You can go on back. Just please try to find out exactly what happened."

"Yes Ma'am."

Emily began to cry the moment she entered the room. Jeremy was seated on a cot, curled up into a ball in the corner. His face was already turning horrible colors and there were blood stains on his chin and cheek. His lip was swollen and dark. The school nurse, Mrs. Turnboldt, nodded to her and quietly exited the room. Emily walked over and took a seat beside her brother. She reached out for him but he shifted further away. Emily slid down closer and put her arms around him. After a moment he began to sob and hugged her to him tightly. They sat that way for a while, until Jeremy's shaking had all but stopped. She stroked his hair away from his forehead and looked into his eyes.

"Who did it?"

Jeremy stayed quiet.

"Did they do anything else to you? Something I can't see?"

His tears began to spill once again and she hugged him close, silently cursing the disgusting town they lived in.

Casey shook her head in disgust. "So did he tell you who attacked him and what exactly they did?"

"No. It was obvious that something terrible had happened to him, I could feel it in my heart as I held him. My parents got there a few minutes later and my Dad went in to speak to him alone. The next thing I knew my Dad said they were taking him home and I should get back to class. I told him they should take Jeremy to the hospital to get checked out and my Dad said it wasn't necessary."

"Do you think Jeremy told your Dad what happened?"

"I really don't know. Nobody said another word about it."

Emily and Shelby were clearly both emotional and Casey decided not to push any further for the time being. "How are the preparations coming along for the harvest festival?"

Shelby smiled. "It's this weekend Casey. Are you coming?"

"Wouldn't miss it."

"Everybody will be there," Emily added. "My parents even decided that we should go."

Casey tried to act cheerful. "Will you be baking Emily?"

"My Mama always bakes at least a few apple pies to sell on the church table. It sounds like she's gonna go ahead and do it this year as planned. I usually help her with it."

"Well, put one aside for me and I'll buy it for Douglas. Apple's his favorite."

"Will do. And thanks for trying to help, Casey. It would be nice for someone to be held responsible for Jeremy. I guess we all should be."

Casey enjoyed the peace and quiet as she drove home. These days her life was pretty hectic, not that she was complaining because she loved staying busy. She was really looking forward to Halloween, and even to the Harvest festival in Jefferson. She had never been allowed to participate in those types of events as a kid and she planned to make up for lost time. She had every intention of trick or treating and carving out a whole bunch of pumpkins. But what she was really looking forward to was attending the Halloween block party with Douglas in downtown Atlanta. With all the hustle and bustle of daily life she didn't get to spend as much time with him as she'd like to, at least not time that didn't involve some story that needed to be edited or investigated. Her cell phone rang and she pushed the button to answer it on speaker.

"Hey."

"Your boyfriend is clean," McAfee said.

"He's not my boyfriend. Just some guy I just met."

"Well, there's nothing there. Clean as a whistle."

"He knows who I am but swears he didn't know when he first approached me."

"I could polygraph him."

Casey laughed and thought she heard amusement in McAfee's voice as well. "That might be a bit extreme."

"Alright, let me know."

"I just left the girls."

"And?"

"The same story about their first day but no new details. Emily says her Dad seemed to want it kept quiet."

"If the kid was sexually assaulted he might have thought that word getting out would just make things worse on him."

"Or just embarrass his father."

"Yeah, or that."

"I'm coming to the festival this weekend. Maybe I'll be able to pick up a little more."

"Bring me back fritters."

"Of course."

Douglas had to admit that he was a bit nervous. Should he ask questions and if so how deep should he go? Maybe small talk was the best bet, keep it on the chill side. And what about before he actually showed up? He wanted to show that he cared without it seeming like he was prying or over-stepping. He caught himself pacing back and forth across the living room and forced himself to sit down on the sofa and read a book. Pretend anyway. When Casey came out of her room she was wearing a very pretty dress, which was rare for her, and it made him even more anxious.

"How do I look?"

Douglas got back to his feet and took a deep breath. "You look absolutely amazing, kid."

"I feel awkward. Maybe I should change."

"Well, you look really pretty Casey."

"You look like you're about to throw up."

Douglas laughed and waved his hand. "Just excited for you."

Casey walked over to him and hugged him tightly. "I'll be fine. Those days are over."

Emma came out from Casey's bedroom towing her gigantic makeup case behind her. "I've taught her at least twenty ways to kill a man. She'll be just fine."

Douglas grinned and shook his head. "Maybe just slap his hand if he gets too touchy."

Casey checked herself in the mirror. "I haven't worn a dress in a little while."

Emma put her arm around Casey's shoulders. "You look gorgeous my peach. Just remember it's no big deal. Keep it low pressure. You like each other or you don't, life will go on."

"Well I'm gonna call you later to tell you how it went."

"Oh, I'm not going anywhere. Douglas and I have a date to binge watch some Netflix till you get home."

"I'm making popcorn," Douglas added.

The doorbell rang and Casey instantly felt queasy. "Gosh you guys, I don't know about this."

Emma placed her palms on the sides of Casey's face and looked straight into her eyes. "It's not a big thing. It's just a little fun. Go on into the bathroom and take a few minutes while we check this cowboy out."

Casey smiled and left the room as Douglas went to open the door. He was met by a good looking young guy who seemed as nervous as Casey. "Hi Sir, you must be Mister Powell. I'm Jerry."

Douglas offered his hand and Jerry shook it firmly. "Good to meet you Jerry. Come on in, Casey will be just a minute."

"Jerry, this is Casey's best friend, Emma."

Emma smiled sweetly as Jerry approached her to shake her hand. "Very nice to meet you Emma."

"Nice to meet you as well Jerry. Please, have a seat."

The three sat and checked each other out.

"So," Douglas said, "Casey tells me you're a finance major?"

"Yes Sir. I've always wanted to go into business and hope to go on for my Master's."

"What year are you?"

"Third, Sir. I'm a junior. I work part time as well doing some light bookkeeping for a housekeeping service."

"How do you like living in the Chatham apartments?" Emma asked.

"Um, I didn't realize I mentioned..."

"We know everything about you Jerry."

Casey interrupted, much to the obvious relief of poor Jerry as she came back out into the living room. "Hey."

Jerry nearly jumped to his feet. "Hi Casey. Wow, you look really nice."

"Thank you. So do you."

"So," Casey looked at them. "I'll see you guys later. Y'all save me some popcorn."

"You know that's never gonna happen," Emma winked at her.

Casey could see that Douglas looked nervous and moved over to give him a hug. "I'll be fine," she whispered into his ear.

"Of course you will. Go have fun."

Jerry offered her his arm and they were out the door. Emma turned to Douglas. "So, should we follow them?"

Douglas laughed. "She'd catch us."

"Right. So, popcorn?"

"Why not."

Casey was a bit surprised when Jerry pulled the car to a stop in front of the Art museum on Peachtree street in downtown. "Is this where we're going? When you said a surprise I wouldn't have guessed this."

"I hope you like museums."

"Are you kidding me? I love them."

"Well it's not just a museum tonight. I chose this special because there is a gothic art exhibit leading up to Halloween and tonight is the kickoff party."

Casey could hardly contain her excitement. "Are you serious! How did you know I would like this?"

"The stack of books on the library table when we met. I saw you were reading a book called Chalice and I looked it up to see what you were into."

"And you found Vampires."

"And I found Vampires," he smiled."

"Well, you just won major points for this one."

"Let me get the door for you."

Jerry hopped out and jogged around the car. Casey felt all of her nervousness and anxiety just fade away as he opened the door and reached out for her hand. She took it and stepped out to the sidewalk with a smile on her face. "Thank you so much for this. I'm really excited."

Jerry beamed. "Oh, but there's more." He removed two black masks from his pocket and handed her one. "Everybody has to wear a mask my dear. We can't remove them till midnight."

"Oh my goodness! An actual masquerade party!"

"You ever been?"

86

"No, never. I can't wait!"

Casey couldn't help but notice how pleased Jerry seemed to be that he'd made her happy. Maybe things were starting to look up in the guy department she thought.

"Shall we go in and meet some vampires, Miss?" Jerry smiled.

"Lead the way Sir."

Jerry made the turn onto highway ninety-two and headed toward Jefferson. Casey enjoyed the beautiful scenery along the way. There were orchards and rustic old barns, beautiful turn of the century farm houses and gorgeous harvest displays welcoming visitors to come after dark for free hayrides and cider. There was something about this time of year that just seemed to connect with her soul. She loved the colors, the foods, the events, the excitement, but most of all, the family environment and community of it all.

"Hey," Jerry nudged her softly. "What you thinking about over there?"

Casey took his hand for a moment. "Thanks for coming with me today."

"Are you kidding me? I love this stuff. Don't even try to stop me if there's a pie eating contest."

Casey laughed. "Oh, I won't. I wanna do it all."

"Halloween's in a couple days."

"I know, I'm excited."

"You picked up your costume for the party with your Dad, I mean your…."

"It's fine. He is like my Dad. I picked mine up but I can't get him to tell me what he's going as. I tried to sneak in and peek but he caught me."

"Well, it sounds like a lot of fun."

Casey smiled at him. "I would have invited you but it's kind of a…."

"A daddy-daughter thing, I get it," he nodded. " It sounds awesome. And so does he."

Casey took a moment to think about that. A Daddy-daughter thing. It was certainly true that nobody had ever loved her the way that Douglas clearly did. He worried about her more than she worried about herself and truth be told, she was the same way with him. The thought of it all made her happy and she was in a perfect mood for a festival as they pulled into Jefferson and searched for a parking spot.

"So, you understand the situation right?" Casey asked.

"Yup, I'm good. I don't know anything about anything. I'm just your arm-candy."

She laughed. "Someone has a high opinion of himself."

"And yet you can't deny it's true."

"So we do our thing, enjoy the festival, try to mingle, and maybe pick up on a conversation or two and try to get a feel for the people. Especially the younger people. If I can get close to Emily's Dad and his groupies so much the better."

"And nobody knows that the two girls met you already."

"Well I met Shelby the first day at the D.Q. But nobody knows I met Emily. It's better if they don't find out."

"What exactly are we listening for?"

"Anything that tells us that they're a town full of bigots, racists, bullies, just overall scumbags."

"I just can't believe an entire town would think that way."

"That's what we're hoping to find out. Keep your cell in your pocket and try to hit record if you hear anything particularly nasty."

The turnout was fairly impressive and the smells were incredible. Even from across the fair you could smell the pies and fritters from the bakery tent. Jerry had reached down and taken her hand as they walked and she had to admit that it felt nice. They had exchanged just a brief kiss the other night after the museum show which had been spectacular. The show, not the kiss. The kiss had been sweet though which was all she was looking for, nothing deep and intense. Certainly nothing too emotionally involved or time consuming. Casey was a busy girl, and on a mission to reach her goals. Short term those goals were to finish Community college as quickly as possible on the fast track program and join her friends Emma and Tasha at the University. They would still be far ahead of her but that was okay, at least they would be able to enjoy a little of the experience as a trio, the way they had always planned.

The fair was country for sure. Georgia country to be exact. There were quilting exhibits and wood carving demonstrations, 4-H and other animal organizations, and of course lots of references to the cotton crop and Apple fritters. They stopped at the girl scout booth and purchased two of the home baked fritters and they were amazing. Otherwise it was very much the typical small town affair. There were carnival rides and game booths along with cotton candy, hot dogs, and even a beer tent that looked to be immensely popular. Casey spotted the bumper cars and nudged Jerry.

"My Mama once caught me making out with a boy behind the bumper cars."

"I'm jealous."

"It got ugly. I thought she might kill me and bury me in the backyard."

Jerry smirked. "My Mom caught me with a girl in my room and screamed at me for a week straight."

"Well what were you doin' with her in your room little perv?"

"I suspect just what you were doing behind the bumper cars."

"I was a lady."

"Well, pretty lady, how about you and I jump on the bumper cars right now."

"You read my mind."

They enjoyed a few of the rides before making their way over to the bakery tent. It looked like there must be hundreds of competitors and non-profit groups selling their treats. They searched around for a few moments until Casey spotted Shelby behind one of the tables with a few other women. She took Jerry by the hand and they headed over. Shelby smiled when she saw her coming.

"Hey y'all. Welcome to the Harvest fair."

Casey gave her a little hug. "It's great. We've already been riding and tasting."

Shelby grinned. "Well you haven't tasted the best until you've tasted ours."

"Alright then. So Shelby, this is Jerry."

"Shelby took his hand. "Hey Jerry."

"Nice to meet you. It all smells so good."

"Well here y'all. Try our fritters."

"I'm fixin' to be fat as one of them prize pigs over there," Casey smirked.

"Don't even girl. We're all gonna be on diets till Christmas."

Casey had to hand it to Shelby and her Mama. The fritters were scary good. Somebody could find themselves addicted to the things if they weren't careful. Since Jerry stayed quiet and kept eating she could tell he agreed.

"Amazing Shelby," she said. "So good."

"Thanks girl. Hey, this is my Mama, Carolyn. This is Casey and Jerry, Mama."

"Pleased to meet you Miss Carolyn," Casey smiled.

"Well aren't you just the cutest little thing." Shelby's mother gave Casey a big hug before moving to Jerry and doing the same. "Hello young man."

"Pleasure to meet you Ma'am."

"Y'all aren't from town?"

"No Ma'am," Casey answered. "Atlanta now but born and raised in Concord."

"Oh, my word I have a cousin in Concord. Cute little town."

Bullshit it is, Casey thought. "Yes Ma'am. It sure is."

"Well y'all take a few fritters with you, on the house. Very nice to meet you."

"Thank you Miss Carolyn. Nice to meet you as well Ma'am."

They spent a few moments chatting with Shelby before letting her get back to her sales work. It had been too much for Mrs. Timmons to work the fair this year Shelby said. But she and Emily had baked a few pies for the Church booth. Casey stopped at their table and was greeted by a plump older lady who was so warm she made you feel like an instant friend. "Welcome young lady. Are you interested in some wonderful pie?"

"It all looks amazing. I'm wondering if you might still have one of the pies Mrs. Timmons made?"

"Oh, let me see dear. Yes, we do have a couple. Would you like one?"

"Yes please Ma'am."

"That's ten dollars, love. I'll get a bag for you."

They had spent nearly three hours at the fair and Casey had school work to finish for Monday. They walked hand in hand back toward the parking area, stopping short when they spotted Jerry's car. He dropped her hand and ran over to it, looking absolutely frantic. The car had been wrecked. The windshield was busted and all four tires had been slashed. Someone had spray painted, "Don't come back bitch," on both sides of the car. "Oh my God," Casey put her hands over her mouth in utter shock. How could this have been done without anyone seeing. The answer came quickly. It couldn't. Whoever had done it had to have brought a lot of attention to himself, or themselves, and anyone passing by either wouldn't or couldn't interfere.

Week Four

Casey was so excited she could barely contain herself. She had worn her "day costume" all day long in school but was home now, changing into her real costume, the one she was wearing to the downtown block party with Douglas. All day long she'd been a pirate, with the bandana, the eye patch and even a hook she'd put on for selfies with some of the other students. But now for the real deal, her Vampira costume, complete with black dress, makeup, and long black lashes. Of course she'd had to grab a nice black wig as well. She was much too blonde to be a Vampire Queen.

Douglas had been in his room for more than an hour. She'd called in to him and wanted to see his costume but he had flat out refused which actually made her giggle a bit. Whatever he'd chosen to be, he was taking it very seriously. It was almost eight and they had decided that if they wanted to park anywhere close to the event they'd need to leave by eight-fifteen. She checked her makeup one last time and went to tap on his door. When he opened it and stepped out she was ecstatic.

"Wow, don't you look like an evil beauty," he said.

"Me? Look at you!"

He had chosen what she thought might be the best Dracula costume she had ever seen. It was clearly not a cheap packaged deal. He wore a crisp white shirt with a high, jeweled collar, black pants, crimson vest, and a long black cape with a gorgeous silk lining. He had applied dark makeup around his eyes and his lips were blood red. He popped in his fangs and snarled at her to her great delight.

"Oh my god Douglas! It's awesome. This is going to be so much fun."

He offered his arm. "Shall we?"

There were several corporate lots which they had generously allowed some local non-profits to use as a fundraiser. They found one fairly close to the party for twenty bucks and walked the two blocks to the event. A band was playing "Monster Mash" as they arrived and the aroma of barbecue and beer filled the air.

Casey took Douglas by the hand and led him into the middle of the dancing crowd, surprised that he didn't resist even a little bit. He was always kind and gentle but rarely let his hair down so to speak. But tonight he began to dance and spin her around and was clearly enjoying himself.

"I'm happily surprised," she said loudly over the music. "I wasn't sure you'd want people to spot you dancing."

"They don't know it's me!" he shouted back.

After Monster Mash, Thriller, and Dead man's party, she decided to give the old guy a break and they headed over to check out the food offerings. They ordered a couple of pulled pork sandwiches and two beers before finding a seat close enough to still listen to the band.

"I'm really happy we did this," she smiled at him.

Douglas reached over and squeezed her hand. "Me too. And we need to do it more. Maybe we pick a certain day each week and find something cool to do."

"Are you asking me to go steady Sir?" She batted her extremely long lashes at him.

"Why yes I am," he winked.

"Well, I accept."

"You hear anything from Jerry yet?"

"No. He hasn't called since the fair. I shouldn't have gotten him involved in any of that."

"You had no way to know what would happen. It was just a fun fair, you didn't even get to ask any questions that day."

"I know, but still. I like him."

"He'll call honey. Just give him a few days to get over the upset. At least his insurance covered most of the damage and the paper is going to pick up any balance."

"Do you guys still think there's enough of a story there?"

"I talked it over with Sammy. We don't know if there's an official discrimination story or not. We have a lot more checking to do with the School and the district. But there's still the overall issue of bullying and bigotry that I think we can expand on beyond the small town angle. For me it's still about a young kid being made to feel so horrible about himself that he chose suicide."

"People suck."

"Yes, they do."

"You know what I'm thinking?"

"What's that?"

"Funnel cake."

"Oh yeah, I'm in. Who's got it?"

After a brief five minute wait on line for the powdered treat, Douglas steered her west, a few blocks down third and then onto Fulton, a busy residential street with house after house decorated for the holiday. It looked like a scene from a movie with jack-o-lanterns, flashing lights, dancing skeleton's, and throngs of happy kids.

"Are we sight-seeing?" she asked.

"Uh, no. We're trick-or-treating."

"No way!"

"Oh yes way. We are not just observers my dear. We're in this."

Douglas produced two plastic pumpkin bags from beneath his cape and handed one to Casey. "We're not leaving till these are full."

"Down this side and back up the other!"

"Lead the way."

Two hours later they collapsed into the patio chairs on the condo balcony and put their tired feet up on the oversized ottoman. They had amassed an enormous amount of candy that they decided to donate to the boys and girls club near the Daily's office downtown. But not yet. First they would pig out on a few of the best offerings and give themselves a major sugar buzz. Tomorrow they'd be crashing about halfway through the school and work day but it would be well worth it.

"I'll trade you a peanut butter cup for the Almond Joy," Douglas offered.

"I'll take that deal. Double actually if you want two."

"Oh yeah."

They sat in silence for a few minutes chewing on chocolate and enjoying the beautiful evening. Douglas took a sip of the coca Casey had prepared for them and set down his cup. "So, I'm glad we have some quiet time together because I wanted to talk to you."

"Sure. what's up?"

"Well, I...Well, here." Douglas handed her a large manilla envelope. " I'll just let you take a look."

"Mysterious," she joked as she took it and opened up the clasp. She slid out the papers and read silently for a few moments before looking up at him. "I don't understand. These are adoption papers."

"Yes."

"They have my name on them."

Douglas took her hand nervously and nodded. "In the State of Georgia Adult adoption is legal and actually quite easy. Especially when the person being adopted is an adult but still under twenty-one. You know how much I love you and already think of you as my daughter. I was wondering what you might think of making it official? If you'd like to, you could legally become my daughter and I would legally be your Dad. That's the most important part but also we could make decisions for one another in an emergency if need be and stuff like that."

Casey stared at him in utter shock, her eyes began to moisten. "You mean...You mean you really want to adopt me?"

"I mean that absolutely."

Casey jumped up and pulled Douglas to his feet, grasping him tightly to her as she cried.

"Does this mean yes?" He tried to breathe.

"Yes! Yes one hundred percent yes!"

He kissed her on the forehead and looked into her eyes. "You just made me very happy kiddo."

"You just made this the best day of my life. And it was already pretty close."

"You realize of course this means I get to ground you."

"You wish. But nice try."

They laughed and embraced again. "Oh my god I have to call Emma and Tasha right now. I can't wait to tell them, they're gonna be so excited. Let me go grab my phone, I'll be right back."

As she ran to her room he felt his own eyes moisten a little too. Who would have thought that first day when he met the very shy, timid, seventeen year old Casey Malone in a prison day room that she would one day be his daughter. But here they were. He took another bite of his Almond Joy and smiled.

"You want me to be your God-daddy?" McAfee asked between bites of his breakfast.

"No thank you," Casey replied with exaggerated sweetness.

"You don't know what you're missing. I could teach you how to fish an' all that."

"Please. I'm a small town Georgia girl. You can't teach me shit. I'll teach you."

Douglas laughed as he buttered his toast. "Back to brain- storming you two. What's our new plan of action?"

"Well, you said Sammy is handling the school district end," McAfee answered. I think you and I should check into any records of assaults, suicides, harassment complaints, even rapes and murders going back say, twenty years. Let's cross our t's and make sure this hasn't happened before. Maybe Malone can try to talk to a few more people. Try to shake something more off the tree."

"I'll try. Not sure if the whole town doesn't know all about me by now."

"Will your boyfriend go back up there with you?"

"He still hasn't called me," she sighed. "But Emma's off today too and she said she'll come with me. She's a better bodyguard anyway."

102

"She's got her concealed carry permit now too," Douglas added.

"Yup. And she's now a second degree black-belt. I'll be in good hands."

"Just watch your six," McAfee grunted.

By ten a.m. Casey and Emma were on their way back toward Jefferson. As usual, Emma was driving like she was rushing to the hospital. "Try not to kill us please," Casey said.

Emma smirked. "Don't you worry my peach. I got this. But let's talk about more important things like new dresses for the ceremony."

Casey smiled. "I still can't believe it."

"Oh, I do. He loves you. The man looks at you like a treasure, Casey. I'm so happy you guys found each other."

"I can't believe it will be a done deal before thanksgiving."

"It's so awesome. Think about it, as bad as your holidays were as a kid and now you're gonna have a real family just in time. I think I'm about to cry."

"Don't you dare. I just put my makeup on."

"I can't believe he gave you an adoption-engagement bracelet. That might be the cutest thing I've ever heard in my life."

Casey looked down at her gold and diamond bracelet. "Ahh, thanks a lot. Now I have to fix my makeup again."

Emma laughed. "You're gonna cry like a baby in court."

"Lord, I know it. Y'all better bring lots of tissues for me."

"I'll be crying right along with you girl, please."

They pulled down Main Street in Jefferson at ten forty-five, too early to speak to any of the High School students but they hoped this time to interact with a few of the shop owners. They parked in front of the post office hoping that it might provide for slightly better security and walked down a short distance to a small antique shop. An elderly couple owned the store and though they seemed friendly and polite they were clearly not interested in engaging any serious questions. The girls checked out a juice bar next and purchased a couple of smoothies from a girl who seemed like she had just smoked a major blunt. She was only barely awake and they were surprised that she was able to function enough to operate the blender.

The next stop down the walkway was a cute little florist and gift shop and Casey decided she'd like to find a nice card and gift for Douglas for what they were now calling "adoption day." She and Emma began reading through the cards and laughing together at some of the sillier ones. A man came from the back room and was instantly friendly.

"Hey y'all. Sorry, I was wrapped up back there getting an arrangement ready for delivery. Can I help you with anything?"

He came over as he asked the question and stopped to look at Casey.

"I know who you are. You're Casey Malone."

Casey never knew how someone might react upon recognizing her. Some wanted a selfie and others were scared to death. The clerk offered his hand and a genuine smile. "I'm Marcus, Marcus Laney."

Casey took his hand and returned his smile. "Very nice to meet you Marcus. This is my friend Emma."

Marcus shook Emma's hand as well and then began to speak in a quiet, almost conspiratorial tone, even though no one else was presently in the shop.

"I know why y'all are here. I wanna help."

"With?" Casey asked.

"I knew Jeremy. I know about everything that poor kid went through."

"How did you know him?" Emma replied.

"Well, he would come in about once a week, just to chat a bit. I could tell he didn't have many friends and needed someone to confide in."

"And he chose his friendly neighborhood florist?" Casey asked.

"He chose another gay man. Maybe the only other person he knew in the world that was gay."

Casey perked up now. "How did he know?"

"Because I put a pride flag up in the window when the parade was happening in Atlanta. Jeremy came in that very day and began to hint at some questions. Once I confirmed, he just let go and started to talk. It was pretty emotional for him."

"When was that?"

"Just this past summer. Before school started up again. But then he began coming in so much I started to pay him a little here and there to help out a bit."

The girls accepted Marcus's invitation to join him for some sweet tea as he finished up some work in the back. He talked freely as they sat and sipped, so freely that they barely needed to ask any questions. He was cutting and arranging some flowers in a large white vase with precise care. "For Mrs. Tinsdale. She passed just the other day the poor thing. Ninety-three years old. She taught elementary school here for nearly sixty years bless her heart."

"Gosh," Emma shook her head. "Sixty years."

"Can you imagine? I'd be fit to be tied after day one, girl."

Casey figured Marcus to be about thirty-five. He was maybe five-ten and wore khaki shorts, a pink polo and sandals. His hair was perfect and his mannerisms so obvious that she had assumed he was gay the second he walked out to greet them.

"Marcus, forgive me for asking, but how is it that you seem to be doing so well in a town that clearly dislikes people who are different?"

"Oh they hate my guts girl. Most of them barely speak to me until somebody gets in trouble with their girlfriend, gets married or dies. I actually live in Smith's Grove so I'm only here from eight till four and out before dark. I want nothing to do with the children of the cotton after that."

"So they really are that bad?"

"Some, but not all. All it takes is one bully and a whole lot of people to be scared of him. In this case it's a bunch of them and they all pretty much run the town."

"Ted Lawson and his crew."

"You'll never see it. They can act as polite as can be. It's more subtle and cunning. Like holding a door for me when no one else is around and saying ladies first."

"What about Jeremy?"

Marcus stopped fidgeting with the arrangement and sighed. "Yeah that was different. Jeremy was a nuisance to them."

"How so?"

"Because I come into town with my lunch in a bag and keep to myself in this store. Jeremy was out and about, in church with them and in school with their kids. He was sitting beside them in class and showering with the other guys after gym class."

"So general homophobia?"

"Like he would infect them, yup."

"Did he talk to you in any detail about what was going on in school?"

"Enough to get me so upset I actually considered trying to report to some higher authorities. I was just so worried that I'd make things worse for him. If I had known...."

"There's no way you possibly could. Would you mind telling us some of it?"

"Of course. Who knows, maybe you can bring some good out of this."

Fridays were always busy in the shop. Marcus did open up on Saturday but only for four hours in the morning so that he could enjoy a bit of the weekend like everybody else. Any flower or balloon order had to be in by Friday for Saturday morning pickup. It was August nineteenth, hot as an oven outside and nobody was in a good mood. He'd spent the day dealing with irate customers who were taking absolutely no joy from their errand running. What everyone wanted was to be sitting in a pool somewhere sipping on a cold drink and wishing they could afford to travel somewhere else for the summer. Marcus didn't know anybody in the County with that kind of dough.

He'd just about finished up his prep for weekend pick-up's when Jeremy Timmons came in the door. It surprised Marcus a bit because he hadn't realized it was that late in the day. But he checked the clock and sure enough it was three-fifteen and school was out for the weekend. It was only a ten minute walk from the High School to Main street but he knew in this heat it had to be brutal just the same. He grabbed a bottle of water from the fridge and told Jeremy to sit and hydrate. The boy looked distraught and it wasn't just from the heat, Marcus could tell. The week before, Jeremy had come in and told him what was obviously just a small part of what had happened on his first day. Marcus suspected that something absolutely horrible had been done to Jeremy but all he could do was listen and offer his support. When Marcus was sixteen he had experienced a sexual assault and he knew that look. The look of inner turmoil when you feel that you've completely lost control not only of your external world but your own emotions and thoughts as well. That look that says I can't find peace within my own soul or block out the voices that would have me believe that I'm of no value to the world.

Marcus had assured Jeremy that he could talk to him about anything, tell him anything, and it would never go any further. To his surprise the boy didn't speak any more about what had happened in school that day but only about his Dad's reaction to the events. Jeremy's parents had been called in to the school and immediately refused any medical help, insisting that they would take Jeremy directly for any treatment he might need. But they hadn't. Instead they just drove him home, leaving him to lay down in the backseat and cry quietly as he listened to his Dad asking what did he expect? How did he think that normal guys would react? Didn't he understand that's what happens when you're a sissy, a punk, a fag, weak? Those boys had done him a huge favor. Maybe now he would learn his lesson, forget about all that gay bullshit and straighten out his life.

Jeremy had begun to stop in quite a bit, clearly hiding out, afraid, Marcus figured, to even go home. Marcus understood all too well how it felt to be despised in your own community, but to be so berated at home? It was all too clear that this kid felt like he couldn't fully relax anywhere. It wasn't uncommon of course, this type of reaction spewed out of parents all over the world, inflicting the most serious of injuries to their kids who were already struggling emotionally. But when it was your Dad hurling insults at you, your Mom? That kind of damage would never be easily undone, if it ever was at all.

Something had happened to Jeremy today though, something new. Marcus could see it. Obviously Jeremy trusted him a little bit. He hoped so anyway. Every teen needs an adult that they can confide in and look to for support. High School was a horrible place no matter who you were. It's a den of predators and their prey, where the mere suggestion of any weakness could earn you a whole world of hurt. It was bad enough to be a less than athletic kid, to be a little nerdy or a book- worm. But to be gay? In Jefferson of all places? These people used the Bible not for salvation, not as a guide for living a deeper and more fulfilling life, but as a weapon of vile and hate. They'd use old testament passages that nobody really understood, while completely ignoring the new testament passages that everyone completely understood. Don't love your brother, stone him. Dish out as much ridicule, judgement, and punishment as you could and somehow this made you a God-fearing and upstanding citizen. And they would call Marcus a pervert, all the while perverting every single truth that they claimed to believe in.

"So, what's going on Jeremy?"

Jeremy kept his head down and shrugged. Marcus stopped his work and pulled up a stool to sit down beside him. "Come on buddy, we're friends. Tell me what happened?"

Jeremy's eyes welled up and Marcus put his hand on his shoulder. "It's just you and me Jeremy, please tell me."

Jeremy wiped his eyes, his answer coming just barely louder than a whisper. "They hate me."

"Who hates you?"

"Everybody."

"I'm sure that's not true. I don't hate you. Just the opposite actually."

"Only because you're like me."

"Like you how? Smart? Talented? Devastatingly handsome?

Jeremy tried to smile. "You know what I mean."

Marcus sat with him quietly for a moment as Jeremy sipped his water and tried to compose himself a bit more.

"I got into school today and it started immediately. They didn't let up for a single second all day long."

"Tell me."

"First I opened my locker and a gay porn magazine falls out with fag written in big red letters across the front. It seemed like everybody had been just standing around and waiting for me to see it. I go to church every single Sunday Marcus, I pray every night. I don't look at porn."

"I understand. The vulgarity was meant to upset you and it did."

Five minutes later I walked into my homeroom class and someone had written, Adam and Eve not Adam and

Steve, across the blackboard. Everyone was pointing at me and laughing until Miss Mason came in and yelled at them to be quiet and take their seats. She didn't say anything to me but she looked at me like I was damaged or something and it just made me feel pathetic."

"Yeah, they've been using the same tired old lines for decades now."

"Oh it went on and on. Every class there was either a message on the board or some crude drawing left on my desk. Everybody seemed to know about it but me."

"I'm sorry that happened Jeremy. I know how it feels."

"It kept going, all through lunch with comments being shouted out, gym class with two of the guys pretending to have gay sex and the coach laughing as he told them to knock it off. You know, like it was his job to stop them but he really couldn't give a shit."

The phone rang and Marcus stood up to answer. Just a customer confirming they could pick up their four dozen yellow roses the next morning. Some ladies luncheon or something. He leaned back against the counter to stretch out his tired back. Jeremy looked up at him, looking emotionally drained.

"You know what was the worst part? About two o'clock I was in the hallway headed to my last class when a girl I recognized from Math walks up to me and smiles. She said what the other kids were doing was horrible and if I ever needed a friend she'd be happy to be one. I felt so much better for a second that I thought I might start crying on the spot. Then she breaks out laughing and shouts out, 'The Freak bought it!' Everyone was laughing."

Marcus walked over and hugged the kid to his chest. He couldn't help but let his mind wander back to when he was in school. Some things never seemed to change.

Casey shook her head in disgust. "So it definitely seems organized. A whole lot of planning went into that day alone and even some staff failed to intercede."

"Fuckers," Emma said. "I can't even imagine."

"I can," Casey sighed.

Marcus nodded. "Me too,"

"I'm sorry guys. I know you can. God, I can't believe people can suck so bad."

"Douglas used to tell me bullying was a disease that seemed to have no cure," Casey added. "You always hear people defend it with, well maybe he's bullied at home or maybe she's had her heart broken and is just lashing out because of her pain. That's all bullshit. Even if those things are true you have no right to be evil to other people like that."

"Well," Emma opened her arms out wide. "What exactly can we do about it? There has to be something."

"I've never heard of anything that works," Marcus answered. "Casey's right. They say education is the answer, anti-bullying campaigns and cheap bumper stickers. But in the end nothing changes. Hate is hate. And there's no church in this town teaching them to think any differently that's for damn sure."

Sammy wasn't in the best of moods, not that she ever was but today was certainly no love fest for the Daily staff. As Chief Editor she took a whole lot of heat from the big-wigs upstairs and shit trickled down from there. If she was getting reamed, then so were you. Right now she was sitting at the small conference table leafing through some papers and ignoring Douglas, Casey and McAfee who all sat patiently waiting. When she finally looked up she seemed almost surprised to see that they were still there.

"So, the School Board attorney sent back a letter that took about ten pages to say fuck you. They have one documented visit to their offices from Mrs. Timmons who voiced concerns about her son being, what they note as, mildly bullied, in school. There are some notes from the school nurse that he came into her office the first day with apparent injuries but never stated the cause of the injuries. They made note that based on the time of day that he may well have been injured at home before he even arrived on property."

"But Emily described the ride into school and seeing him enter the front door. He was fine then," Douglas answered.

"They'll argue possible abuse at home and that the sister might be lying."

"He wasn't treated well at home but Emily hasn't said anything about physical abuse," Casey added.

"Look," Sammy slapped the papers down on her desk, "We got into this with the idea that it was a breaking lawsuit against the district for failure to protect. There's nothing there."

"Nothing on record as far as previous incidents or arrests either," McAfee agreed.

"We've got some investment in time and resources already," Douglas said. "So let's go with human interest. We'll stay away from any possible lawsuit and just stick with the story."

"If we can prove bullying there still may be a possibility for an arrest," McAfee offered.

"So far it's a whole lotta hearsay," Sammy sighed. "His Dad is the biggest pile of shit in the story so far."

"I'll keep trying," Casey said.

Sammy nodded. "Just be careful Malone. "These are the most dangerous stories, when reputations are on the line."

She turned to Douglas. "Get this wrapped up. People will be interested but it's not front- page. Get it done."

Fifteen minutes later Casey, Douglas and McAfee were taking their seats at the taco place just down the block. They ordered a family tray of tacos and a few sweet tea's. "Extra hot sauce Please," Casey added as the server took their menus.

"Must be nice to be young and have a gut of steel," McAfee smirked.

"If you can eat prison food you can eat anything," she replied.

"So this one is bothering me," Douglas looked out the window and shook his head.

"This is a fourteen year old who was bullied so badly he saw no way out but to kill himself. And somehow we just can't seem to pull the story together."

"You wanna squeeze the Dad?" McAfee asked.

"Oh you bet your ass I do. But not yet. We'll talk to that fucker last, after we've gotten everything else together. Casey, I want you to press Emily a bit more first. There's no way the damn florist knows more about what was happening at home than she does. I wanna know everything she knows. I don't give a shit who called us, if he's responsible for this then let's take him out."

"What about you and me?" McAfee asked as the tacos arrived. "A few more napkins please honey, thanks."

"You and I are going to squeeze the other locals about the gang of bullies while Casey works on the kids some more. Sammy will lose interest soon so we need to pull this all together."

Casey crunched into a taco and answered with her hand in front of her mouth as she chewed. "Do you guys think there's really a chance of an arrest?"

"It happens," McAfee answered. "Just recently a woman got charged after bullying her boyfriend to kill himself. Cyber bullies have been charged for the same but not always successfully."

"I just don't get why Mister Timmons called you if he's one of the guys that was doing the bullying. What's he up to?"

"My guess is that he's torn," Douglas answered. "That's certainly no excuse. But I'm thinking he was getting it pretty bad himself over having a gay son."

"So instead of being a man he took it out on Jeremy as badly as the rest of them."

"Sounds like that's probably the case," McAfee agreed.

"Well eat up," Douglas said. "We'll do our best to get this kid some justice."

Casey made plans to meet up with Shelby and Emily at their regular spot in Smith's Grove. The ride was beautiful but after making the trip several times it was starting to get old and Casey talked with Emma on speaker phone to pass the time.

"I can't believe he's being such a little bitch about it," Emma was saying. "So they messed up his car, big deal. You're gonna lose out on dating a beautiful girl because of it?"

"I'm sure he's never experienced that kind of shock before Emma. I mean, I'm used to some rough shit but I think he's lived a pretty sheltered life. Maybe his folks want him to stay clear of me."

"Well he needs to man the fuck up and grow a pair."

Casey smiled. "What about you? How many guys have asked you out lately that you've shot down in flames?"

"It's not the same. You two already had something started."

"Yeah, a little but not really. It's not like I'm heartbroken or anything."

"You want me to fix you up with one of them?"

"Don't you dare. I wasn't looking for anything to begin with. Jerry approached me."

"I'm surprised he had the balls."

119

Casey laughed again. "I'm gonna call you on my way back so you can keep me company."

"Okay my peach. I'm just sitting here pretending to study anyway."

It was just past three when Casey pulled into a space close to the gazebo. She wasn't expecting to see the girls until three-thirty or so and decided to rest her eyes a bit while she waited. She lowered her window to enjoy the fresh air and leaned back against the headrest.

Casey was skipping and humming to herself as she made her way home from school. Things hadn't been too bad today, just the normal mean looks and a little bit of name calling here and there. A couple of the other girls made fun of her dress and told her that their grandma's wouldn't even wear it. They told her no boy would ever like her because she was far too ugly and nobody could ever kiss her nasty face without throwing up. But compared to some days, today had been a breeze. She was looking forward to reading the final chapter of her book and maybe even starting a new one. Something sinister was going on with Ramon, more so than usual. He wasn't like the other vampires, he'd abstained from drinking any human blood and devoted himself to helping would-be victims avoid the monsters in the shadows. But lately he'd been acting a little shady, like maybe he wasn't all that innocent after all.

She reached her house and made her way inside. It was pitch black, strangely so for the afternoon, and the lights weren't working. She flicked the switch on and off a few times but nothing happened. She felt her way along the wall to the hallway and tried the switch there as well but still nothing. She thought she heard someone else breathing but thought it must be her imagination playing tricks on her. Her Daddy was working second shift and Mama was out playing cards and drinking with her friends like every day. As she neared her bedroom it seemed like the darkness became deeper and deeper. She reached around the doorframe for the light switch but couldn't find it. She heard the breathing again and began to feel really frightened. Her Daddy's voice came up suddenly from behind her. "Where you going, you little whore?"

A hand landed on Casey's shoulder and she jumped, pushing into the car horn on the steering wheel.

"Sorry! Sorry!" Shelby stepped back and gave Casey a moment to wake up.

"Sorry girl. You were out cold. I didn't mean to startle you."

Casey's heart was racing and it took her a moment to register where she was.

"Gosh, I didn't even realize I was that tired. What time is it?"

"Three-twenty. What time did you get here?"

"Just about twenty minutes ago. Where's Emily?"

She climbed out of the car and gave Shelby a hug, just then noticing a girl she did not know standing beside her.

"She couldn't come. Her Dad is being a jerk or something. But this is Claire. She wants to tell you some stuff too. Claire, Casey, Casey, Claire."

"Hey," Casey offered her hand and Claire took it. "Hi," she smiled.

"Wow, so I guess I could use some coffee."

"Good idea," Shelby agreed. "Back to the cute cafe?"

"Absolutely."

They decided to take seats inside, it was still relatively early in the day and a bit too warm to sit outside on the patio. They ordered three coffee's and decided to try a few slices of the chocolate cheesecake too.

Casey smiled. "So, thanks for coming Claire. You knew Jeremy?"

Claire seemed a bit on the shy side. She would make eye contact but only fleetingly and would play with her hair as she spoke. A bit like Casey did herself when she was nervous. "Yes, I knew him pretty well, and Emily too."

"I guess y'all grew up together. I suppose everybody knows everybody."

"Pretty much. When we were kids we used to go over to each other's houses and stuff. The twins were always together."

"Pretty common for twins that age I bet."

"I guess."

"What was Jeremy like?"

"He never wanted to play with the other boys, only with us. Back then it didn't make any difference to us but Mister Timmons didn't like it at all."

"Did he say something?"

"If he caught Jeremy playing with us he'd yell at him and tell him to get along and play like a boy."

"But he'd come back?"

"Always. Even at that age we understood that he was sad about it and didn't seem to fit in."

"What about later on? Junior High maybe?"

"I think maybe he hoped that if he came out that people would stop trying to force him to be something he wasn't. But instead it seemed like the whole school, the whole town even, turned all their hate on him. People were so horrible to him."

"Would you tell me a little of it?"

"Okay. There were a bunch of things that I saw but the eighth grade dance was the worst."

They had all decided to meet up at the Timmons farm to take some pictures before the dance. Claire had been asked to the dance by a sweet boy named Kenneth who didn't talk all that much but seemed nice enough. His parents had picked Claire up on their way out to the farm and the two of them had sat silently in the backseat together, unsure of what to say and feeling as awkward as could be. Claire was relieved when they finally pulled up at the farm where at least the other girls would be there to talk to. Clay Shephard had asked Emily which was no surprise at all because she was gorgeous and he was the most popular boy in their class. Jeremy had asked Kelsey O'Hara which surprised everybody a bit since he had just recently announced to everybody that he was gay to avoid the awkwardness of the whole dance thing. Kelsey was kind've a nerdy girl, much more into books than spending time with the other kids and all about science and math. She looked pretty in her dress though and Claire told her so which made Kelsey smile just a little. The six of them had stood first as a group and then in couples to have their photos taken by the adults. Shelby arrived a few minutes later with Dwight, who she agreed to go with but really wasn't into all that much, and her parents, Mister and Misses Lawson, who were going to be chaperones along with Mister and Misses Timmons.

Mister Timmons had shaken Mister Lawson's hand and the women had all hugged one another. Right when they arrived it was Jeremy and Kelsey's turn to have their picture taken and they stood together by the railing with open fields back behind them. Jeremy looked miserable.

"Put your arm around her waist boy," Mister Lawson called out.

"Go on now," Mister Timmons said. "She won't bite you, right Kelsey," he winked.

Kelsey smiled politely and moved a little closer to Jeremy who placed his hand on the small of her back.

"Come on now!" Mister Lawson called out again. "Put your arm around her son, what's wrong with you?"

"He's fine Ted," Mrs. Timmons intervened. "They're just kids, they're all a little shy."

"If you're sure that's all it is but damn, the other boys ain't like that."

"He's fine," she retorted a bit more sharply.

"Put your arm around her properly!" Mister Timmons barked out. "I'm getting sick of this bullshit now!"

"That's enough!" Mrs. Timmons warned her husband. "No more pictures, just leave them be."

Mister Timmons pointed his finger at his wife. "I'm not raising no damn pansy and I don't take orders from you. Jeremy, put your arm around that girl 'fore I whoop your fuckin' ass."

"Damn right!" Mister Lawson whooped out like an immature fool.

Jeremy was clearly fighting to hold back his tears as he did what he was told and Kelsey reached down to take his hand reassuringly. "It's okay," she whispered.

"There you go! Shit!" Mister Lawson sneered and looked proud of himself. Mrs. Timmons looked absolutely enraged and Emily was already wiping away tears. Shelby looked mortified but Claire knew she would never open her mouth or she would get it too. She saw Mister Timmons and Mister Lawson exchange nods like they had just accomplished something great and then they were all ushered into two of the cars to head for the school gymnasium.

Casey shook her head in disgust. "So Emily's Dad really did treat his son pretty horribly."

"Oh gosh yes," Claire nodded. "He was awful. I know he's been out pointing fingers but the truth is that he was the worst of them to Jeremy."

"Sounds like Shelby's Dad has a lot of sway over him."

"Him and everybody else. I have never been able to figure out why people care so darn much about what the barber thinks. Sorry Shelby."

"No, I understand. You need to tell it."

"He's a Deacon too right?" Casey asked.

"In title only. He barely even goes to church. Just shows up when there's a camping trip or one of the festivals. Pastor's scared to oppose him too."

"So what happened at the dance? Were things any better?"

"Oh lord no. Poor Jeremy couldn't catch a break at all."

Kenneth's parents had headed back home but Mister and Misses Lawson and Mister and Misses Timmons had volunteered to chaperone. Claire had assumed, correctly so, that it was Mister Lawson's way of being able to control everything and everybody. He walked around the decorated gymnasium with his chest puffed out and a smug look on his face and she wanted so badly to walk right up to him and slap the arrogance right outta him. She turned to see Shelby looking her way but Shelby averted her eyes in obvious embarrassment. Claire wondered how it felt for Shelby to have the biggest jackass in town for a Dad. But as far as Claire was concerned, there wasn't a real man in the whole damn town. None of them had the guts to stand up to this guy, this nobody, that somehow controlled everything from the town council to eighth grade prom. It was absolutely ridiculous and bordered on pathetic. Even her own Dad had stayed quiet back at the farm and she knew very well that he didn't approve of treating anyone that way. It wasn't like Mister Lawson was a great big guy or anything either, he was maybe five-ten and she could probably kick his old ass herself if she wanted. Maybe she would, she thought, put all these grown men to shame.

Kenneth came over to her, looking bashful, and asked her if she'd like to dance. She forced herself to smile politely, though she was inwardly pissed as hell, and accepted his outstretched hand. None of this was Kenneth's fault after all, he was just a boy and she could understand the boy's being afraid to challenge Mister Lawson. How were a bunch of fourteen year old's gonna stand up to the guy when their own Dad's were scared shitless of him.

"You look really pretty," Kenneth smiled.

Claire tried to focus. Kenneth was trying really hard here and she had, after all, agreed to be his date. "Thanks Kenneth. You look really nice also."

"I feel bad for Jeremy. That was messed up."

"Yeah, me too."

Mister Lawson was making his rounds about the room and he passed by Claire and Kenneth. "Atta boy Kenny. That's how you do it."

"Fuck off asshole." The words had escaped Claire's mouth before she even knew she was talking. Mister Lawson stopped, smirked, and then just went on about his way without any comment.

"Holy shit Claire!" Kenneth laughed and looked back over his shoulder to watch Mister Lawson walk away. "That was awesome."

Claire grinned. "He deserved it. How much you wanna bet he calls up my Dad to tattle like a little girl."

"No doubt. Will you get in trouble?"

"I dunno but it was worth it. I feel great."

Kenneth laughed again and suddenly Claire felt like her night might not be a total shit show. But the feeling only lasted for about ten minutes.

Kenneth had asked her if she'd like punch and cookies and she had told him she'd love some. She really couldn't care about punch and cookies but her southern manners dictated that she politely accept the gentleman's offer to bring her some. That's what her grandma said anyway and who was she to argue. He was being nice and that's all that mattered. She took a seat on the bleachers with some of the other girls including Kelsey and she took Kelsey by the hand. "You okay?"

"I'm fine. I just feel bad."

"Where's Jeremy?"

"Probably hiding somewhere and I can't blame him."

"Wanna dance with me?"

"Yeah?"

"Yeah, come on."

The two girls marched hand in hand out to the dance floor and danced to what the D.J. had called his magic mix. They were laughing and having fun when Kenneth passed by with the refreshments. "Oh, I'm coming Kenneth."

"Stay and dance you two," he smiled. "I'll wait for you."

"He seems really sweet," Kelsey said.

"Yeah, he does. Sorry that your date isn't working out like you thought."

"Well, I knew what was what. I just didn't expect it to get so ugly."

They were still dancing a few moments later when Mister Timmons approached.

"Girls, where's my son?"

"I think maybe the bathroom," Kelsey lied. "I'm sure he'll be right back."

"Has he danced with you at all tonight Kelsey?"

"She's dancing with me right now Mister Timmons," Claire answered. "If you don't mind."

"I do mind. And watch your smart mouth or I'll get your Daddy on the phone right now."

"You're ruining our dance Mister Timmons. Please leave us alone."

He stormed off quickly in search of Jeremy and the girls knew things were about to get worse. They walked back to the bleachers and sat down next to Kenneth who looked just as concerned. "Everything okay?"

"No," Kelsey answered him quietly, "I don't think so."

They couldn't see exactly what was happening at first, only that people had stopped dancing and some were actually gasping in surprise. But through the crowd came Mister Timmons, yanking Jeremy along beside him by the back of his collar, so forcefully that Jeremy's shirt had come untucked and he looked as if he might be choking a bit. Mister Timmons didn't release him until they had reached the bleachers and stopped right in front of Kelsey.

"Now you ask this nice girl to dance and stop being so goddamned rude and disrespectful."

"Mister Timmons...," Kelsey started to intervene.

He held up his hand for silence and looked so enraged that she was afraid to say any more for Jeremy's sake.

Mister Lawson made his way over and stood just a few feet off looking very satisfied. Like a snake that caught himself a big fat mouse. His wicked grin made Calire's stomach turn and she was about to speak up herself when Kelsey suddenly grabbed Jeremy by the hand and led him away to the dance floor.

"SOMETHING SLOW!" Mister Lawson shouted at the D.J.

As the softer music began to play Claire saw Kelsey pull Jeremy's head to her shoulder and even under the dim lights she could tell he was crying. She couldn't help herself and began to cry as well, allowing Kenneth to put his arm around her and pull her into him.

"That lying fucker." Casey was pissed. "He fed Douglas and Lloyd a real bullshit story about how everyone else was responsible for Jeremy's death. But it was him, wasn't it?"

Claire nodded. "Mostly, I suppose. But lots of people were involved, not just his Dad. I saw it a lot at school and the men in town treated him like a leper."

"Did Emily witness all of this?"

"Yes but it's hard for her, you know? I mean, it's her Dad. And he treats her really well."

"Cause she does what's expected."

"Right."

"How did all the other kids react to what happened at the dance?" "It was humiliating for him. Everybody was snickering and pointing. That's how it always was with most of them."

Casey hadn't been surprised that Shelby sat quietly as Claire told the story. Her Dad certainly looked like the

132

bully he was and she must feel embarrassed to be associated with him.

"None of this is your fault Shelby," Casey reached out and took her hand. "You can't control what a grown man does, especially when he's your own father and has that much authority over you."

Shelby suddenly looked very sad. "I just feel so ashamed of him sometimes, and my brother too. And my Mama just paddles along like an obedient dog and never says a word."

"Is she afraid of him?"

"Not physically, but if she ever says anything he doesn't like he berates her for hours. I suppose it's just easier to keep quiet."

"Does he treat you like that?"

"He never really talks to me that much at all. A couple of times I told him to leave my Mom alone and he just told me to mind my own business. He and my brother are thick as thieves though. My brother models himself after my Dad and tries to bully everyone."

Casey took a sip of her coffee and looked out the cafe window toward the gazebo.

"I didn't know Jeremy, but I know he didn't deserve to feel so hopeless that he killed himself."

The girls stayed silent, and Casey signaled the waitress for the check. "Thank you both so much for meeting me again but I gotta go. I'm meeting up with my friend Emma to do some dress shopping."

Claire smiled. "Big date?"

"Nope, I'm getting adopted."

The ride home was even more boring than the ride up. Emma was having an early dinner with her folks and then the two girls planned to meet at Macy's and try to find something that Casey could wear for the court ceremony. It was still two weeks away, but better to be prepared early than to panic at the last minute. The two lane highway passed through miles of apple orchards and small family farms and the scenery was really quite beautiful. She tried to clear her mind and appreciate it all but a pickup was tailgating so closely that it was making her nervous. The driver clearly wanted to pass but the road twisted quite a bit and you would literally be taking your life in your hands to try it. The speed limit was fifty and she was doing fifty-five and she wasn't about to speed up just to make some jerk happy.

About seven miles out of town they hit a relatively straight stretch and the truck swerved out quickly to come around her. It sped by quickly and she felt relieved to finally be rid of it. But suddenly it came to a screeching halt directly in front of her, leaving her no time to react. Casey slammed on the brakes and fishtailed out a bit before sliding off the road into a small gulley. The car jolted to a stop in the tall weeds and her head lurched forward. Fortunately she was able to stop herself before connecting with the steering wheel and getting hurt. She took a second to try and slow her pulse down before unsnapping her seatbelt and opening the door. She felt hands on her and thought at least they had the decency to stop and make sure she was okay. But suddenly she felt herself being pulled out roughly and she instantly knew that this had not been an accident. She reached back into the car trying to grab for the pepper spray in her purse but it was too late. She found herself thrown up against the outside of the car facing two masked men who began throwing punches without a word. The blows to her belly sucked the air right out of her before they started in on her face and head. Pain seared through her and she fought to regain her breath but each time she thought she'd catch just a small bit of relief they'd land another powerful shot to her ribs. She began to fall but they pulled her back up and continued the onslaught. As she felt herself slipping into unconsciousness she wondered if she was about to be raped.

Casey awoke in a panic, not knowing where she was or if she had been taken. She knew she was in a bed and tried to sit up, only to feel searing pain shoot through her side, forcing her right back down again. She heard someone approaching quickly and fear suddenly gripped her. But seconds later she was looking up into the very worried face of Lloyd McAfee. He hovered over her and spoke to her very calmly, in his practiced cop voice. "It's just me Malone, you're safe honey."

"Where am I?" It hurt to speak and her mouth was dry. McAfee grabbed the plastic cup and straw from the bedside table and held it for her to take a small sip of water.

"Atlanta General. You got here about twenty minutes ago. Douglas is on his way. I was closer."

"There were some guys…"

"Do you know how many? Or what they were driving?"

"Two, I think. Masks. An old Ford pickup...gray."

"Okay, that's good. Try not to talk anymore for right now. The pain meds will kick in soon."

She nodded and closed her eyes again.

When she awoke Douglas was holding her hand and looking more worried than she had ever seen him. He leaned forward and touched her cheek softly. "Hey."

"Hey."

"You've been playing tackle football again."

"You caught me." Breathing hurt. She felt every breath in and every breath out and she knew the feeling all too well. "Cracked ribs again."

He squeezed her hand a little. "Yeah, three. The good news is your organs all look okay."

"How's my face look?"

"You're gorgeous."

"Worse than prison or not as bad?" She spoke in a whisper, trying to control the pain.

"Well, no broken fingers this time so that's good. But you took some good shots to the face, I won't lie to you."

"Great. Can't wait to go to school."

"Did you recognize them at all Casey? Maybe their voices?"

"They didn't say one word. Just beat me up."

"Lloyd said you think just two of them?"

"Yeah."

"Tough guys. Two of them on one petite girl."

"Last time I got beat up we had pizza."

Douglas smiled. "You want some pizza?"

"I want some more pain meds. And then I want pizza."

Week Five

McAfee parked in front of Ted Lawson's barbershop and he and his two buddies climbed out of the car. The three men had been friends for years, more than thirty years for one of them and at least twenty for the other. They had all been on the job together, but Charlie retired five years back and Jake about three. They still got together for backyard barbecues or at least to grab a couple beers once a week. McAfee was six-two and Charlie towered over him. He had taken up serious weightlifting right out of the academy and he was built like a tank. Jake stood about six foot, the opposite of Charlie with a beer belly he was very proud of and an appetite for barbecue. All of them wore sour expressions on their faces.

When they entered the shop Ted Lawson was just finishing up with a customer. He blew the hair off the back of the man's neck with the handheld hair dryer and removed the smock. He nodded to the men as they entered. "Detective."

Three others were seated in the chairs along the wall, the regular ass kissers McAfee thought to himself. He made note that the guy in the corner was one of the local cops, just in case the boy got any stupid ideas.

McAfee stood silently for a moment and surveyed the room, his friends stood behind him glaring at the barber. The customer handed Lawson a ten, told him to keep the change, and beat it out of there. McAfee turned his attention to the other three men. "Y'all take off too."

The young cop smirked. "I don't think so."

McAfee walked slowly over and stopped in front of the man. He shifted uncomfortably in his seat. "I wasn't asking, boy."

Lawson waved his hand a little, trying to calm things down a bit.

It's fine fella's. Y'all go on and grab somethin' to eat. I'll catch up with you later."

The young cop stood up and stared straight into McAfee's face. "You sure Ted? Cause this ain't nuthin' to fret over." He stepped a few inches closer.

"One more inch," McAfee growled. "Please."

"Now now, now now fella's." Lawson came over and placed his arm around the young cop's shoulder, gently guiding him toward the door. ""Let's not get all puffy."

The other two men left as well and Charlie planted his massive frame right inside the door.

"So, Lawson," McAfee walked slowly across the shop looking everything over. "You own a gray pickup?"

Lawson shook his head. "No Sir, no I surely don't."

"I know you don't. Anything I ask you I already know the answer. How about your punk-ass kid?"

The barber went to say something but seemed to think better of it. He waited a moment before answering. "You already know that we don't. Wanna tell me what this is all about?"

McAfee took a seat and crossed his legs. Charlie and Jake remained standing with their eyes fixed in a death stare on Lawson who looked more and more nervous by the second.

"You know what it's about Lawson. Don't try to bullshit us."

"Look, Detective…"

"Retired. No longer under anyone else's authority. You might wanna keep that in mind."

Jake reached over and twisted the rod to close the front blinds, the barber looked as if he was close to a full on panic attack.

"Sit here next to me Lawson," McAfee pointed to the next barber chair.

When he was seated, McAfee could see the man's hands beginning to tremble.

"Tell me something, Who are these two tough guys who beat up on a defenseless young girl?"

"I don't know what you're talking about."

"Oh, come on now. This ain't my first rodeo son. I can see it in your eyes that you're full of shit. Give me the names. Tell me who the gray truck belongs to."

Lawson shook his head but stayed quiet.

"Let me break a few of his goddamn fingers," Charlie snarled.

McAfee leaned forward, close to Lawson. "I'm gonna find out boy, and when I do, and I tie them to you...Well, we will be back here. You fucked with the wrong girl."

The barber was trembling so much he didn't even try to maintain eye contact. McAfee sat for another moment before getting up and walking out the front door with Charlie and Jake. Ted Lawson got to his feet and grabbed a bottle of whiskey and a shot glass from a drawer and poured himself a drink, with some difficulty, and needed both hands to raise it to his lips. He grabbed his cellphone and dropped himself back into the chair. He found a number in his contacts and pushed the button, raising the phone to his ear. "Yeah, it's me. We need a full meeting."

"Let me help you get your legs up," Emma said and gingerly lifted Casey's legs up onto the bed. "There you go, you need another pillow?"

"No, I'm good. Thanks Emma."

Emma sat down on the edge of the bed beside her. "Anything for you my peach."

"So much for dress shopping."

"I know your size and your style and I will find it for you. Don't you worry about a thing."

"I'll look great with two black eyes and a bruised jaw."

"Thank God they didn't break your nose."

"They were surprised it wasn't, just bloodied."

"Small favors."

"Yeah."

"I should have gone up there with you Casey. I'm so sorry girl. This wouldn't have happened if I was there."

"It's not your fault Emma. Nobody saw this coming. I mean I was just hanging out with two High School girls."

"You think one of them set this up?"

"I don't think so, but all it would take would be for Shelby's brother to follow her."

"I hear Lloyd scared the devil outta their old man."

Carry grinned. "I would've loved to have seen that."

Emma laughed. "I wouldn't want Lloyd that pissed at me."

"That's for sure."

"We all really love you Casey."

Casey took her by the hand and smiled. "I love you guys too. That's all that really matters to me now."

"Well, young lady. You need to rest. I'm gonna hang out and study till Douglas gets home. Just shout out if you need me."

"Okay, thanks Em."

"Salad tonight?"

"Hell no, tacos."

"Forgot who I was talking to. Tacos it is."

Douglas sat in Sammy's office watching her pace back and forth, her usual habit when she was upset, stressed, sleep deprived or just plain pissed off like today.

"I should give McAfee the nod to dismantle their whole damn town."

Douglas nodded. "Think of that lawsuit."

"Shut up. Nobody asked you to be reasonable. Why aren't you angry? It's your kid for fuck's sake."

"Oh, I'm angrier than I've ever been. I already beat the shit out of my pillow and I'll admit I cried a few times the last couple days."

Sammy finally slunk down into her chair. "So what now?"

"Look boss, this is obviously more than a little bullying right? I mean, it has to be. Nobody goes this far without trying to cover something up. They're showing their hand."

"Covering up what, that they're bullies?"

Douglas shook his head. "I know you wanted this wrapped up but this is personal now. I need some time to get to the truth."

"I want Lloyd with you every time you go up there. Got it? No exceptions."

"You have my word."

"I already told him we'll contract his retired cop friends too if need be."

"I appreciate that Sammy."

"How's Malone today?"

"Sore, but her appetite always stays in place."

"I wish I had her metabolism. I have to live on Kale and low cal dressing while she's packing away the burritos."

Douglas smiled. "You're coming to the adoption party right?"

"Wouldn't miss it."

Douglas stopped to pick up the massive taco order on his way home and found Casey sitting up in the living room with Emma and McAfee when he arrived.

"Hey, good to see you up and about, kid." He leaned over from behind the sofa and kissed the top of her head before dumping the bags on the kitchen counter.

"How are you feeling?" He asked.

"I'm good," she smiled, "Better now that the tacos are here."

"Casey's always happy when you feed her," Emma laughed.

"Well, I got beef and chicken tacos and I got a couple large orders of the nachos too. So dig in everybody."

They ate in the living room with plates resting on their knees, listening to the thunderstorm that had moved in quickly and was now pounding the sliding glass doors. Douglas was pleased to see Casey up and about. The swelling had gone down around her eyes but they remained black and purple with a jawline to match. It broke his heart that the kid had suffered yet another severe beating and this time he felt one hundred percent responsible for it personally. He should have never sent her up there in an investigative role even if she was just meeting with young girls outside of Jefferson. He just could not shake the feeling that there was more to all of this than met the eye and he had no intention of dropping it now. Someone was going to pay for what had happened to Jeremy and now to Casey, no matter what it took.

"Any more hot sauce?" Casey asked.

"Yeah catch," McAfee tossed her a couple of the small packets.

"So, what now?" He asked. "There are way too many gray pickups in the County to go door to door and we don't know who all the players are to start checking registrations against names."

"How about Danny Lawson's friends?"

"All the boys that Casey met at the DQ that first day and their folks come up with nothing. No gray trucks."

"Damn," Douglas leaned back in his seat. "Ideas?"

"Can't we all just search different parts of town till we spot it somewhere?" Emma suggested.

"Too many barns and too much private land that you can't see from the road," McAfee answered. "But I'd bet they have it stashed for now anyway. They know Casey can I.D it."

"I wonder if Shelby or Claire heard anything about it?" Casey shifted in her seat slowly to take pressure off of her aching ribs. "Or Emily for that matter. Maybe I should reach out to them. Text maybe?"

"We don't even know if they were involved," Douglas answered. "For all we know they set you up."

"I don't get that feeling. I think somebody followed one of them there to meet me, probably Shelby since I was meeting Claire for the first time. But now that they came together to see me they may both be in some danger."

McAfee massaged his forehead. "What a damn mess. This has all really taken a turn sideways.

"I think Casey's idea is all we've got," Emma wiped her mouth and crinkled up her taco wrapper. "Make contact and if they don't know what happened maybe they will feel shocked into finding something out for us. I mean, they sound nice enough, they might not be happy that Casey was hurt like this."

Douglas nodded. "Alright, Text Shelby and let's see."

"On second thought," Casey nodded, "Let's let them see my banged up face in person."

"No, I don't like that," Douglas shook his head.

"You know what though," McAfee leaned forward. "Between all of us and my boys we could keep watch in all directions and see if our gray truck shows back up. It would be great if we could make an arrest for Casey's assault and then try to squeeze them for information on Jeremy."

Douglas was shaking his head but Casey reassured him. "I'll be perfectly safe Douglas. Matter of fact you can be in the car with me. We can try to meet them closer to the city, someplace that McAfee can assure full coverage and hopefully catch these guys. Otherwise we may never get them."

"What about your ribs, honey? You're still in pain."

"I'm wrapped up good and I'll be in pain either way. At least I'll have a chance of getting these fuckers."

They met up just north of the city line, in the parking lot of a Cracker Barrel just off the highway. Shelby came without the other girls this time, and she smiled as a boy Casey didn't recognize pulled into a space right next to Casey and Douglas. She climbed out of her car and opened the rear door of Douglas's mercedes to slide in behind him. Casey wasn't able to shift to speak to her so she adjusted the vanity mirror over the visor to see her better.

"Hey girl."

"Oh my god Casey. Are you doing better?"

"It's not as bad as it looks. At least not as bad as it was."

"I'm so sorry that happened to you. I asked around but nobody seems to know anything about a gray truck. Which is funny cause lots of folks must own gray trucks so you'd think somebody'd drop a name or two."

"You'd think."

"I know this is bad, I just can't believe somebody would do this over the Jeremy situation. Are you sure it wasn't just a random road rage thing?"

"I'm sure. This was planned and personal. Guys don't just go running around in ski masks like that."

"True."

"Shelby, this is Douglas. You two haven't met yet."

"Pleased to meet you Sir."

"Nice to meet you Miss Shelby. Thank you for taking the time to help us."

"To be honest, I'm just looking to make sure my Dad isn't blamed for all of this. I know he's rough around the edges and can't stop running his mouth but he'd never actually hurt somebody."

"Well, we're not accusing your Dad or anyone else," Douglas answered. "I assure you we are just trying to find out why Jeremy would feel the need to resort to such tragic measures. This is a really horrible situation when a kid that young feels that unhappy."

"I know, It makes me really sad to think about it."

"Who's the boy?" Casey asked.

"Oh, that's Gordy, we kinda date a little. I drive a little bit when it's close to town and nobody cares but for this far I needed someone with a license."

"Oh, did he know Jeremy?"

"Just by name, he's older than all of us."

"So have you spoken with Emily?"

"Her Dad's been on her about her grades and stuff. He won't let her out of the house on school nights but she said to tell you she's sorry you got hurt."

"I really appreciated how y'all are trying to help."

"Yeah, Claire said to tell you hey. She couldn't make it today. There's a big planning session for the Thanksgiving food drive at church."

They decided to go on into the restaurant for some pie and invited Gordy to join them. The boy was quiet and uninterested, sitting at the table with them but paying no mind whatsoever. He kept himself occupied behind this phone screen and only looked up to scoop another bite of his pie.

"We keep going in circles," Casey sighed. There's something here and we just can't seem to get hold of it."

"We need to find out who drives the gray pickup," Douglas added. "That's the key to everything."

"I can't think of anyone else to ask," Shelby answered. "Nobody knows anybody with a gray pickup."

"Chief Willie's got a gray pickup," Gordy mumbled from behind his screen.

"What?" Claire reached over and gently lowered Gordy's phone. He rolled his eyes just slightly. "Chief Willie's got a gray pickup."

"Wille Charles?" Douglas leaned forward. "Chief of police Willie Charles owns a gray pickup?"

"Yessir."

"How you know that?" Claire pressed.

"Cause over the summer he paid me and Donny to help him haul a couple cords of firewood back to his place from a farm in Marietta and we used his gray pickup. He don't drive it that much cause he takes the patrol car everywhere."

They sat in stunned silence for a moment.

"Son of a bitch," Douglas finally said.

Gordy went back to his phone screen. "What y'all care about that old crappy truck for anyway? Most of the time Chief Willie just keeps it back there in his barn. It runs like shit."

"Are you're sure it's gray?" Casey asked emotionally.

Gordy looked up at her. "I went to kindergarten, girl. I know my colors."

Shelby and Gordy finished off some pie and sweet tea while Douglas and Casey quietly pondered the reality of the police Chief being directly involved in her assault.

"Does Chief Willie have any kids?" Douglas asked.

"Two," Gordy answered. Willie Junior, we just call him Junior, and Donny."

"How old are they?"

"Willie's twenty-three, he's away in the army, and Donny's my age, seventeen."

"Are you boys friends with Danny Lawson?"

"Kinda. I know all those guys. Danny, Mike, Jessie."

"Are you tight with them?"

"Nah, not really. They all kinda stick to their own group. But they're cool mostly, a little over-competitive and they like to prank people."

"But you are friends with Donny, The Chief's son?"

"He mostly keeps to himself but I know him, sure."

"Gordy, did Shelby tell you about what happened to Casey?"

"Yeah," he looked at Casey, "Sucks."

"It does suck," Douglas nodded. "And it's some bullshit for two grown guys to beat up on a defenseless girl wouldn't you agree?"

Gordy took a sip of tea from his straw. "Yeah, that's messed up."

"Do you think Donny could have been involved in such a thing?"

"If Chief Willie told him to."

"Without question?"

"If Chief Willie says to do it, Donny's gonna do it."

They walked back out to the cars and Casey took Shelby aside for a moment.

"Gordy seems nice."

"He's fine, for now."

Casey grinned. "Gotcha. But this was really helpful, thanks."

Shelby smiled. "I'm really sorry they hurt you. The guys in Jefferson are all just assholes. If you don't agree with everything they do or say this is what happens. And I know my Dad is the worst of them, he's the one that gets everybody else all riled up. But I don't believe he would ever physically hurt someone like this."

"But he has it done." It wasn't a question and Shelby knew it. She frowned.

"I hope he didn't Casey, but I really don't know for sure."

They exchanged a quick hug and Casey took her by the hands. "I know it's rural Georgia girl, but maybe you keep letting Gordy do the driving."

"I'm fifteen Casey, I have my permit."

"Right, still."

"Shelby laughed. "It's like having a big sister, I like it."

They were halfway home before they spoke.

"The police Chief had you attacked."

"Sure looks that way."

"So badly you needed to be hospitalized."

"Yup."

"With broken bones."

"Yeah."

"I don't believe this. What in the hell is going on here?"

"Something more than a gay kid being bullied. It has to be. They don't like any of us sniffing around."

"So it's a good bet that Donny is one of the attackers. I'd guess both brothers if one wasn't away in the service."

"Maybe he's not. Leave maybe?"

"We'll check that out. But if not my first guess is Danny Lawson."

"Shelby's own brother."

"If so I don't get the feeling she knows."

"No, me either."

They were interrupted by Casey's cell phone ringing. "Hey."

Casey listened for a few moments. "Okay, meet us at home, we have some answers."

She hung up and turned to Douglas. "McAfee checked with everybody. No sign of the pickup in any direction."

"So they didn't follow Shelby. At least not today."

"We really don't know who Gordy is."

"We need to get on the pickup before they move it. I'll talk to Lloyd about it back at home. We have a very small window here to tie your attack to the Chief."

They sat out on the balcony enjoying the early November air and soft evening breeze. Casey and Douglas had spent the last hour discussing everything from Jeremy's case to the adoption party and even their Thanksgiving plans. Douglas had suggested that perhaps they take a three day trip to Savannah for the holiday, just the two of them, and the idea made her smile. "So a soul food thanksgiving this year?"

"How awesome would that be?"

"Uh, very awesome."

"Some good ol' southern comfort food."

"Yes Sir. I'll wear a proper dress with a lacy collar and you can wear a suit and a white Fedora being as it's Savannah and all."

Douglas laughed. "We can sit out at a sidewalk cafe and stroll through the squares."

"Yup, sit out at the cafe sipping coffee like Hemingway and browse the shops down on river street."

"This is all sounding really good."

"We doing it?"

"I'm in if you are."

"Are you kidding? It's gonna be awesome."

"Christmas here at home though."

"Oh yeah. Got to."

"I have big plans for this year."

"Do you?" She smiled. "Can't wait."

The doorbell rang and Douglas left her to continue jotting down party notes on her legal pad. When he came back out he was followed by Jerry who stood there looking sheepish, holding a bouquet of red roses in his hands. Casey looked at him but said nothing.

Douglas clapped his hands together once. "Um, so I'm just gonna leave you two to talk."

He made eye contact with Casey who nodded slightly that it was okay. When Douglas had gone back inside she pushed out one of the patio chairs with her toes. "Have a seat."

Jerry sat down and looked hard at Casey. She could see the shock in his eyes.

"It's not as bad as it looks. Bruises always look their worst just before they start to fade away."

"Gosh Casey, I'm so sorry, for everything."

"Don't be. It's fine...I'm fine."

"No, it's not okay at all. I was just freaked out by all of this and I'm not used to this kind of stuff."

"I'm not either Jerry. I felt really bad about what happened to your car but I had really thought we liked each other. I know I liked you."

Jerry leaned forward and finally handed her the flowers. "I like you too Casey, I'm so sorry for being stupid like that. I've been thinking about you non-stop."

"My phone number is still the same Jerry."

"I know, I know. I'm dumb. What more can I say? I'm really sorry. I hope we can start over."

Casey shrugged. "Well, you should have brought me some chocolate instead of these girly flowers."

Jerry grinned. "I'll go get them right now, just say the word."

She rolled her eyes playfully. "You're already here so you might as well stay."

Jerry took her hand and seemed to finally relax a bit.

"Who told you about what happened anyway?" She asked.

"Emma. She texted me and called me about fifty names and then told me."

Casey laughed. "Sounds like she let you off pretty easy."

"I agree."

He glanced down at her yellow pad. "Party menu?"

"Would you like to come to my adoption party?"

"Kind of you to invite me."

"I haven't invited you. I just asked if you'd like to come."

Jerry laughed. "You're really gonna make me work for it aren't you?"

"Oh, you bet your ass." She smiled. "Of course you're invited to my party."

"Then I would be very honored. That's the truth."

They sat for a moment and listened to the sounds of the city.

"We're going to Savannah for Thanksgiving. It will be our first father-daughter trip. Wow, that's the first time I said that out loud."

"You're beaming. That's really great Casey, congratulations."

"Thank you. I'm really very happy."

"You ever been before? To Savannah?"

"Once as a kid and then with Douglas just after I was released from prison. He took me on the river cruise and out to the beach for a few days."

"Sounds like it's becoming your special spot."

She smiled. "I guess it is."

"So how 'bout as a kid? You go anywhere for the holidays?"

Casey shook her head and Jerry immediately regretted asking. He could tell that a painful memory had been triggered. "I'm sorry, it's none of my business."

She took his hand. "No, it's fine. If you really wanna know who I am then these are the stories you need to hear.

159

Maybe then you'll understand why it's so important for me to help anybody else that I possibly can who's being abused. The reason I'm willing to take these risks, Douglas too."

Casey always liked to ride her bike through Aiken park, along the back trail, past the pond with the ducks and small walking bridge, and out the other side into the East end of downtown Concord. The wooded trail opened up directly to Delaney Street near Miss Shea's bakery and the bait and tackle shop where all the men sat around drinking beer and talking about the damn politicians. Just down the way Misses Sweeney ran court over the hair salon where the women all talked about the men and their beer drinkin' and general uselessness. Now and then Casey would stop in and Misses Sweeney would give her a big hug and a lollipop and always say the same thing to her. "Girl, when's your Mama gonna bring you in here so I can get into that gorgeous hair of yours?" Then she'd tell Casey to hop up into one of the chairs and she'd brush out all the knots while she talked to the other women about Mister Sweeney, the most useless of all men, she'd say, and how if he ever fixed the garbage disposal she'd might drop dead on the spot from the shock of him finally doin' somethin' worth somethin'.

Casey always hugged Misses Sweeney and all the other ladies goodbye, sometimes hearing them whisper what a poor child she was for havin' to live with that drunken fool

Seth Malone. But it was no matter to Casey cause she knew they were right and if she had her own way she'd be living far away with another family. After all, that was most of the reason she liked riding her bike so much, she felt free to go where she wanted and talk to people who were nice to her for a change instead of just yelling at her all the time and shoving her out of the way.

Mama used to never let her ride further than the end of the street but now that she was nine she was allowed to go further as long as she wasn't gone too long and made it back home in time for supper. One time she was fifteen minutes late and Mama sent her to bed without any supper and by morning her stomach was growling somethin' awful. So now, she made real sure to keep an eye on the clock tower in the center of town and leave in plenty of time to stay out of trouble.

Mister Claiborne would always welcome her into his book store with a warm smile and he never minded if she sat herself down cross legged on the floor and read for a while in the children's section. Today she was excited as she entered the store and marched right up to the counter. "Is it here Mister Claiborne?"

"Ah, Miss Casey, it sure is, young lady, and I'm waiting for you to review it for me."

He walked her over to the kids mystery shelf and pulled down the brand new Nancy Drew book. "There you go Missy, set yourself down a spell and check it out."

She was so excited she could barely contain it. She was always very careful not to break the binding or crinkle any of the pages or else Mister Claibrone wouldn't be able to sell it and he'd lose money. She didn't want him to get upset with her and maybe not let her come in anymore. She held the book gingerly, like a treasure, and entered back into the world of her favorite heroine. Nancy was smart and strong and even the boys knew not to mess with her. And you couldn't just go around stealing things or robbing people because Nancy would catch you even if you had a really good plan. Today she fell deep into the mystery of the missing prize diamond, wondering how somebody could have stolen it from out of the locked safe in old lady Treadmont's mansion. She was snapped out of her trance as a family entered the store and the bell rang out from over the door.

"Merry Christmas Mister Claiborne!" they called out happily as he went to offer assistance.

Casey looked up at the clock over the front counter and her heart nearly stopped. It was four-fifty and she had promised to be back home by five. The ride was at least twenty minutes if she went really fast and it wasn't easy to go really fast on the trail without taking a spill. She ran to hand the book back to Mister Claiborne.

"Thank you, Sir. I have to go or else imma be late and get in trouble."

"Well, that's for you Casey. You keep that one for yourself as a Christmas present. Merry Christmas sweetie."

Casey froze in place for a moment and looked at the book in her hands and then back to Mister Claiborne. "A Christmas present for me?"

"Of course, you're one of my favorite people."

A wide smile spread across Casey's face. "Nobody ever gave me a Christmas present before."

Mister Claiborne suddenly looked very sad. She didn't know why but sometimes grown-ups were just hard to understand. He patted her head and smiled down at her. "You go on and run along now before your Mama gets upset."

"Thank you Mister Claiborne!" She dove into the man, hugging tightly into his side before running out the door and onto her bike. The basket would come in handy to hold her new book and she couldn't wait until after supper to keep reading.

She made good time back through town and was onto the trail by five. But five wasn't good enough and she knew it. She was already late and couldn't go much faster on account of the trail being a little slick from the drizzle earlier. But the more the minutes ticked away the more panicky she became until finally she was pedaling full force and nearly to the opening of the trail close to her house. She would have made it fine were it not for a patch of deeper mud that caught her tire just right and sent her sliding down into the yucky mess. She wasn't hurt 'cept for her pride but her dress was destroyed. Mama was gonna have a breakdown for sure. Fortunately her book had landed on the grassy patch running alongside the trail and wasn't damaged at all. He bike was covered in the mud though and so she'd have to walk it the rest of the way home and wash it off with the hose tomorrow. She hoped that maybe since it was Christmas eve that Mama might be in a better mood and not be too mad. Those hopes were quickly dashed.

By the time she walked through the side door it was five-thirty, and hard as she tried to quickly wipe the mud from her shoes she managed to track some right onto Mama's linoleum floor. She knew it was gonna be bad as soon as she saw her Mama's face.

"What in the world did you do now! You look an awful fright!"

"I'm sorry Mama, my bike slid in the mud and I fell."

"That damned bike! You ain't got no business ridin' that thing around in the woods to begin with. You are not a goddamned boy! And wearin' a dress while you're doing it too!"

"But I always ride with my knees close together like you said Mama."

"I don't care about your goddamned...good lord look at your knees all scraped up too!"

"Get in the shower right now and leave me that dress. You better hope I can get that clean. We are not made of money."

"Yes Ma'am."

"And what's in your hand?"

"Mister Claiborne gave me a present?"

"Give it here."

"But Mama…"

"I said give the damned thing here."

Her Mama looked the book over for a moment as Casey stood watching in a silent panic.

"Why'd he give you this?"

"He said I'm one of his favorite people."

"I bet. What's he some kinda pedophile or something?"

"I...he owns the bookstore Mama."

"You know what a pedophile is?"

"No Ma'am."

"It's an old goddamned pervert who likes little girls instead of grown women."

"But Mama, he never…."

"I said get your ass in the shower."

"Yes Ma'am. But can I please have my book to read it later."

"You're not keeping any old perv's book. Go on before I get Daddy's belt. And don't even think about supper. Shower and bed."

"But it's Christmas eve Mama. Can I please just read it before you take it?"

"You got three seconds to get outta my sight."

Like every Christmas, there were no carols or decorations, no tree or presents. She had known even as a little girl that there was no Santa. She tucked herself under her covers and clutched her only doll to her, staring out her window into the night sky and trying to make out some of the constellations. It was nice to be given a Christmas present, even if she only got to keep it for a little while. She didn't want to have to tell Mister Claiborne what happened so maybe she just wouldn't go into the bookstore for a while. She knew Mama was going to forbid her to go back anyway. She wondered what was happening in all the other houses in town. Were they hanging ornaments and stockings or making a nice big dinner? Maybe they were going to bed early so that Santa would come and leave them loads of wonderful presents. She turned away from the window and closed her eyes, hoping that maybe she wouldn't feel as hungry when she was sleeping.

Jerry started to say something but stopped. She gave him a little smile but he seemed unable to return it.

"Don't feel bad Jerry. It was a long time ago. I'm only telling you so that you understand my motivation. Having this opportunity to work with Douglas and for the Daily means I can try to help other people who are bullied or abused or discriminated against and that means a lot to me. If it hadn't been for Douglas doing that for me I'd still be on the inside and probably for life."

"I do get it, and I'm really sorry for ghosting you like that. I just wasn't used to being in that type of situation before."

"And I understand completely if you don't want to risk it happening again. But I would really appreciate it if you would decide now. If we're moving forward and growing closer I don't wanna wake up to a note on my pillow. I need to try to move on without any more loss for a while."

"If you don't mind I'd really like to stick around, Casey. I really have been thinking about you a lot and wishing I hadn't disappeared like that. My sister told me I'm a dumb ass."

"Sounds like she and I will get along just fine."

"Oh, I'm sure you will."

"Well, I'm happy you're back. I really like you."

Jerry leaned forward for a kiss and she found herself hoping that he was as sincere as he seemed.

McAfee watched through his night vision binoculars as Charlie moved expertly toward the barn, keeping low and moving quite stealthily for his massive size. Jake kept steady watch on the Chief's house as McAfee covered Charlie.

"Still clear," Jake whispered.

"You're good to go Charlie," McAfee affirmed into Charlie's headpiece. The big man gave a thumb's up from just outside the barn door before proceeding to open it very slowly, an inch at a time in case of creaky hinges. Once he had the space he needed, he slipped inside to the darkness. The other two men waited in the silence with eyes fixed on the house and barn. After a moment Charlie's voice came into McAfee's ear. "The masks are on the seat of the truck. I've got a few pics and some shots of the truck."

"Okay, clear out."

"Copy that."

Charlie came back out the barn door and closed it as slowly as he had opened it before once again keeping very low and heading back to the others. He got on on his belly and elbows between them.

"Gray truck, two masks, black gloves."

"Motherfuckers."

"Yeah."

"What's your move?" Jake asked.

"Surveillance. How many guys have you got?"

"The two of us and we got Reggie Sheen also. Three shifts around the clock."

"Okay, perfect. The Atlanta Daily's got you guys approved for payment. We've got one week so hopefully we see something we can use. Video anything and pics as well. I'll get with Douglas and see if we can't maybe stir the pot a bit."

Douglas woke early and found Casey already up and reading one of her favorite novels, Night Visitors, on the sofa. She was already fully dressed and her backpack was resting on the coffee table all set to go.

"You going to school today?"

She looked up and nodded. "Yeah, I'm feeling pretty good and they've been very patient already."

"Well the Dean said under the circumstances you can take all the time you need."

"I know, but it's not the same working from home. I'm getting cabin fever. And thanks to Tasha's makeup expertise you can barely see the bruises on my face."

"I can't see them at all. As long as you're sure."

"I'll be fine. I made coffee."

He walked into the kitchen and poured himself a cup. "You want some eggs or something? You should at least eat so you have some energy."

"Just a bagel maybe if you're having one. Don't fuss just for me."

"Bagels sound good. I'm on it."

"Any news from McAfee?" she asked as she walked slowly over to take a seat on one of the kitchen barstools. Her ribs were aching but she kept it to herself.

"They've got a few days left on the approved budget. You know Sammy, she wants the guys who hurt you as badly as we do but a dime's a dime."

"Of course. This isn't the only story in town."

"I just feel like we're finally close to a breakthrough."

"Yeah, but what exactly are we breaking through to?"

"So, you and Jerry?"

Casey smiled. "We'll see. I invited him to the party."

"It's gonna be great, I'm excited."

"Me too. And Savannah will be perfect."

"Can't wait. We need a break."

"I was thinking, how much vacation do you have saved up?"

Douglas laughed. "Uh, probably ten years. I hardly take it."

"We should do a little road trip. Make it back here by Christmas. Check out the Christmas lights in Charlotte, Raleigh, maybe even down in Saint Augustine."

The bagels popped up in the toaster and Douglas plated them, passing one to Casey. "You know what, that does sound pretty great."

"I can do some research."

"Okay. let me know what you find, but let's do it."

"Cool."

Douglas came back around the counter and pulled up a stool next to her. "I've never done one of those carriage rides. I bet that's gorgeous at Christmas."

Casey's face lit up. "Oh wow, that would be awesome."

"Check that out also. All those towns have them but see who's rated the best."

She made a note in her phone. "A week?"

"Make it ten days."

"Wow Mister Powell. You sure you can stay away from the job that long?"

"You sure you can stay away from Jerry that long?"

She laughed. "Please. Right now he's lucky I'm even talking to him."

"We need to make a pact though. We have to try the pecan pie in every city we visit."

"Goes without saying. And if they don't have really good hushpuppies we leave immediately in disgust."

Douglas grinned. "The ones with powdered sugar."

"We're gonna get so fat."

"Nope, lots of walking to see the lights each evening." He checked his watch. "Gotta go. Sammy wants an early update before she heads out to some conference and then I'm meeting with a man named Riley Daniels who's an expert on suicide and violence in the gay community."

"Oh, what's that for?"

"Background for the article. I thought some perspective might be in order."

He kissed the top of her head as he put on his suit jacket. "Best place for a carriage ride. Don't forget."

Douglas was early to the office but nobody was ever earlier than Sammy. Her position as Major stories Editor pretty much mandated that she be a control freak, minding, adjusting, supervising and manipulating every single little detail until the Atlanta Daily produced what she considered to be a worthy experience for its readers. Then the process would begin again as the next edition was prepared. He found her pacing back and forth in her office reading copy, making sure she got in her minimum ten thousand steps for the day. He placed a cup of coffee on her desk and took a seat to wait. After a moment she looked up from the papers and nodded toward the cup. "Double shot?"

"Of course."

"What time's your source getting here?"

Douglas checked his watch. "Fifteen minutes. He's got an hour for me before he has to head out to the airport for a lecture in Chicago."

"Okay, I'm in with you. My morning workshop got cancelled."

"Sounds good. We can decide on a general direction for this thing."

"My initial thought process is to go national and discuss some of the cases from around the country and then delve in more personally to Jeremy's story for a personal touch. How's that sound to you?"

"I think that's perfect. I just hope we can get a little more information before I have to get the final copy to you."

"The boys are still sitting on the pickup?"

"Yeah. Lloyd's hoping to have somebody to squeeze for information."

"How's Malone?"

"Back to school today."

"No shit? That's great."

"She's tough."

"You ready to take the adoption plunge?"

"Never more ready for anything in my life."

"Sooner or later we're printing that story. I hope you know that. The public will eat that all up."

Douglas smiled. "I'm not above opening up my private life to sell more papers."

"Maybe a Christmas article? Feel good shit."

"That reminds me, I need ten days off. Casey and I are doing our first family road trip to see some Christmas sights."

"Oh fuck yeah. We're definitely writing this up. It's printing right before Christmas so take good pics."

Professor Riley Daniels arrived right on time and was escorted into the conference room to meet Douglas and

Sammy. Sammy sent an intern to fetch him some coffee and politely offered pastry which he declined. He was a distinguished looking gentleman, as one might expect a renowned lecturer to look, with impeccable, three piece suit and sharp pressed white collar. His manner was warm and approachable and Douglas found himself wishing Casey had been here to meet him as well. The girl seemed convinced that all academics were assholes.

"Thanks so much for agreeing to meet us, Doctor Daniels."

"Riley, please. And you're quite welcome. This sounds like an important piece and frankly the subject needs all the attention we can bring to it."

Douglas nodded. "Of course. I can tell you that it's been one of the more disturbing cases I've ever investigated and we're not even certain of all the details yet."

"I read the notes you sent me. Teen suicide in the gay community is not at all uncommon. The tragedy is that we have yet to move the needle at all on any real action."

"Can you give us some statistics, Riley?" Sammy asked.

"Of course. As I'm sure you know, the suicide rate has been climbing significantly over the past decade. About fifty-thousand people die by suicide each year but there are actually more than one and a half million attempts. Now, middle aged white men are the highest percentage of those but young people from ten years old to about twenty-four are the second most prevalent. Of that group, the majority are gay, lesbian, bisexual or trans. It's difficult to pinpoint that percentage exactly because we know that many teens commit suicide because they fear what their parents or friends might think of them if they come out. They see themselves as damaged and unworthy to go on."

"What do we know about those influences on kids who do come out?" Douglas asked.

"Well, we know that kids from rejecting families are ten times more likely to attempt suicide than kids from supporting or at least accepting families."

Sammy got up to begin pacing, as she usually did when she was deep in thought.

"What about bullying in school?" She asked.

"It's a major factor," the professor answered. "Bullying and harassment are usually always involved. Forty percent of LGBTQ kids who end their own lives were bullied on school property. Thirty percent were cyber-bullied as well. With all of that stress at home and at school, while also dealing with the pressures of just being a teen and navigating through life, these kids are five times more likely than their heterosexual peers to commit suicide. And when you consider those younger kids from ten to fourteen may not even be sure yet of their sexuality you can see the fear factor involved as well."

"They see what other people go through," Sammy replied.

"Yes. Often- times right there in their own school."

Douglas made a few quick notes and checked his list of questions. "Can you tell us a little about assaults on gay people in America?"

"Sure. As many as two hundred thousand members of the LGBTQ community are victims of hate crimes each year. Now, the official numbers do not reflect that and are in fact much lower."

"Why is that?"

"A number of factors. Fear of retribution, of having to speak out in court, of being outed to family, friends or employers."

"Can you tell us about a few of the cases you've been involved with?"

"Certainly. The suicide that's stayed with me the most was a twelve year old boy named Darby in Wisconsin. This was only a few years ago. He had decided that since the orientation of nearly everybody on television was so easily accepted that it must be that way in real life as well. Sadly, this just isn't so. He was angrily rejected by his parents, especially by his Dad, and his sister took to calling him names like freak and faggot. She was only a year older and they attended the same school."

"I can already see where this is going," Douglas shook his head.

"Right. She went in the very next day and some pretty horrible things around about her brother and pretty soon the poor kid found himself under attack from all sides."

"What was the school's response?"

"There wasn't enough time. They never heard a peep about it. Darby was dead three days later by his own hand."

Sammy shook her head in disgust and took her seat again. "So, in this case we have a combination of things. School bullying including an apparent sexual assault, a hateful response from at least one parent, and intense pressure from the community to conform. We're talking about a small town where everybody knows everybody and so when the trash talking starts they all jump in."

Riley nodded. "Not uncommon, sadly. And this is why so many of the hate crimes go unreported as well. Bashings outside of gay bars, workplace and cyber-bullying, sexual battery, employment discrimination, spiritual shaming, it goes on and on and reaches into literally every nook and cranny of our society."

"Have you seen things improving at all over time?"

"No. Again, if one accepts the Hollywood narrative as reality we would have no issues at all. But as Darby found out, the truth is far uglier than the screenplays would have us believe."

"One last question, Professor. Young adults account for what, fifteen percent of suicides each year?"

"Yes."

"And of those perhaps half are gay?"

"Yes."

"And of those, how many are by hanging?"

"Hanging deaths have increased over the past ten years or so as well, including for teens. But the percentages are still fairly low. It's much more common to see a firearm death or drug overdose. Rough numbers though, seven percent of teen girls and three percent of boys."

They thanked the Professor for his valuable time and Douglas promised to send him a copy of the final article. Sammy checked her watch. "Okay, I gotta run."

"There's a lot here to explore."

"I agree. And it needs to be done. Get as deep as you can on Jeremy's case and I'm gonna take it up with the powers upstairs. Maybe we can go front page again, major feature."

McAfee was flat on his belly beside Charlie, careful not to move an inch as he watched the small group come out of the Chief's house and walk back to the barn.

Once they were closer he held his binoculars up for a better view. The Chief swung open the barn doors on each side before climbing into the gray pickup and pulling it out. His son, Donny, closed the doors before he, and a young woman, climbed into the cab with Chief Willy.

McAfee lowered the lenses and shook his head. "Hello Chief. Hello Donny. Hello Miss Shelby." He watched as the truck drove slowly off the property and another vehicle pulled in behind it to follow. McAfee raised his binoculars again to get a good look at the second driver. "Well, well. Ted Lawson. The whole gang is here."

He dialed his cell and raised it to his ear. "Yeah, it's me. They're about to dump the truck. Don't lose them but be careful not to spook them either. We're running for my car now."

Week Six

It really was quite pretty to watch the sun begin to rise up over the cotton fields. There was almost an ethereal feeling to it, with the gorgeous colors of the morning spraying their light over the pure white cotton as far as the eye could see. Here, just off in the distance in a long abandoned barn, Jeremy's life came to an end. He had chosen a serene spot, a beautiful spot, but Casey was very certain that there was no peace in his troubled heart in the final seconds before kicking that ladder away. Her mind went back to her friend Paulina who had died in the same tragic way. She felt a single tear roll down her face and she wiped it away. She felt a hand on her shoulder and turned to offer a weak smile to McAfee.

"You okay Malone?"

"Yeah...no. It's just really horrible. How can people be so cruel to each other? What's the reason Lloyd? What do they get out of that?"

"Hell, girl. I've been asking myself that question my entire life. Some of the things I've seen…" He shook his head and looked out over the field. "I bet this place was special to him."

"You think he came here a lot ?

"I would bet on that. Probably a place he used to reflect a bit."

"To hide."

"Yeah, maybe."

"It felt safe for him."

"I can see why."

"You think she's gonna show?"

"Yup." He turned to look at her. "You sure you'll be okay with this?"

"Y'all did your part. This part's mine."

"Slow an' easy like we talked about."

They sat in silence for another ten minutes until Shelby's car finally came into sight. She came down the dirt drive and pulled up beside them. She climbed out, shooting a quick but hesitant smile to Casey. She and McAfee climbed out as well to greet her.

"Hey, girl." Shelby moved forward as if to hug Caey but seemed to change her mind, trying to read Casey's expression. "Everything okay?"

Casey nodded her head in McAfee's direction. "This is my friend, Detective Lloyd McAfee."

Shelby offered her hand and he shook it. "Miss Shelby."

"So," she looked suddenly uncertain if not outright nervous, "why'd you wanna meet up out here?"

"We found the gray pickup," Casey answered.

"You did? Oh, that's great. Where is it?"

"It's hidden in the woods out by the old Rivera farm," McAfee answered. Not too far in from the creek but past the old rock wall by just a bit."

Shelby was clearly nervous now. She had gone pale and she seemed to not know what to do with her hands. They were in her pockets, then out, then in her belt loops. "Did you say hidden?"

"Yes Miss, hidden."

"By who?"

"Four people."

"Sir, I…"

"Oh, Miss Shelby. Before we go down that whole road of question and denial let me just inform you that I'm not asking anything, I'm telling. In the car I've got a manilla envelope full of photos of you, your Dad, Chief Willy and his boy, all conspiring to hide evidence of a serious felony.

Maybe more than one but we'll see when they get the truck back to the lab."

She looked as if she might break down any moment as she turned to Casey with a pleading look in her eyes. She went to say something but didn't seem able.

"You played me," Casey said. "All of your stories and heartfelt memories. You gave me just enough to imply that some of the folks in town were mean but never more than that, right? But not you. And who else is behind all this hate? Emily? Her Dad? Your friend Claire with her awesome story-telling skills?"

"You've got it all wrong Casey."

"Oh really? So you weren't with my attackers as they stashed the truck they were driving the day they assaulted me? You weren't the one to tell them we were looking for the truck in the first place? You haven't been spoon feeding me a bunch of fucking bullshit for weeks now?"

"No, Casey. Everything I told you is true. Yes, okay, I told them about the truck after you mentioned it, but I didn't know until after the attack that they had been planning to hurt you."

"Who exactly hurt her?" McAfee asked.

Shelby kept silent and McAfee shook his head. "Sweetheart, you're in a whole world of shit right now. Felony assault, attempting to destroy evidence, plus a list

184

of other assorted pearls that we haven't even begun to unstring yet."

"Does Emily know or not?" Casey asked.

Shelby shook her head slowly. "No."

"Her Dad?"

She shook her head no again.

McAfee leaned back against the car and loosened his tie a bit. It was a nice morning, relatively cool at seventy degrees, but he hated the damn thing choking him all the time and when he was aggravated it always seemed worse.

"Honey, I'm fixin' to put you away for ten years."

The shock of it registered instantly on Shelby's face, McAfee's expert timing and absolute confidence in his words making her go a bit weak in the knees. She leaned back against her car for support and he knew that he had her.

"A pretty young thing like you in the joint? Lord above. They're gonna eat you alive in there, girl."

Her tears came now, the fright of it overwhelming her and making her tremble. McAfee knew when to pounce, and the force of it startled even Casey who had no idea what was coming.

"WHO MURDERED THAT BOY!" McAfee shouted.

"No...No, Sir!" She sobbed,

"THIS WILL BE THE LAST FRESH AIR YOU EVER BREATHE!"

He backed off for a moment, wiping the rage induced sweat from his brow with his pocket handkerchief. Then he nearly whispered. "You'll do. Fuck it. I'll just let you take the fall for the murder."

Panic overcame Shelby, her eyes betraying her and confessing before her lips even parted. "No!"

"Tell us who killed that little boy," he responded calmly.

"I wasn't there," she gasped. "I just...know."

Casey was in a state of shock herself. Had McAfee known it was a murder all along? Did Douglas know? She tried to read McAfee but knew that was impossible. The guy had been a cop all of his adult life and a Detective for more than twenty years.

McAfee dabbed at his forehead a bit more. "Y'all think you're special. That's where you went wrong. Nobody is. I've put away teenagers," he glanced quickly at Casey, "I've put away mobsters. I even bagged me a serial killer one time. You stupid-ass country hicks never had a damn chance. We already had you, but now you geniuses go on and try to hide evidence in the pure daylight. Not that it would have mattered. We've been sittin' on y'all twenty-four-seven."

"I didn't do it, Sir. I've never hurt anyone."

"Truth is," McAfee gazed around at the field. "I couldn't give two shits if you did or not. The four of you dumped the truck, the four of you can go down for murder too."

Casey stayed quiet and let McAfee do his thing. The guy was good, that's for sure. It brought her back to that night outside the trailer when he and his partner interviewed her. But he'd been a bit uncertain with her, presuming her to be a victim and not the one who pulled the trigger. She had been small, still was, and young. He wanted her to tak, to tell him she'd been attacked, violated, that she needed to defend herself. But she hadn't said a single word. Not until she had a lawyer. That wasn't because of McAfee. She'd found him likable from the start. His partner, however, the one who looked like a heavyweight bodybuilder, he was a dick. She knew Charlie had been helping McAfee with this and she told him to keep the asshole far away from her. McAfee had simply nodded.

That night was as clear in her mind as if it were yesterday. First, Jimmy, the one guy she trusted, and cared for, tried to rape her with his grungy buddies. Then he made the fateful choice to come at her with that bat. She'd killed him to save herself. A person had a right to live. After a lifetime of abuse and neglect, of rape and emotional torture, she'd been off to prison. As bad as it sucked it was still a relief. She knew she'd probably get raped on the inside eventually, she was tiny and blonde and though Emma had taught her a bunch of self defense moves that only helped if it was one on one. But then Douglas had come along, he was confident and assertive and so sure that he was going to make things right. And she hoped that it would be true, and it was.

Not everything was peaches and cream. Life simply wasn't fair and if you ever found somebody who truly loved you then you'd better hold on tight because most of the world couldn't give a shit. And now her future was hopeful but also restricted. She was still a convicted felon. She would never be a teacher, or a lawyer, or a Doctor. She would never be a foster parent or adopt a child or volunteer as a big-sister. She would never be allowed to work in law enforcement or become a Counselor or go to nursing school. Thank goodness she loved to write. The chance that the Atlanta Daily had promised to provide meant everything to her. That paper, and all of the love and acceptance they'd shown her, was her future, and Douglas himself was her heart.

Casey met McAfee's glance for just a moment and he offered the faintest, wry smile. He'd given Shelby a few moments to let his words sink in and ponder a life behind bars. She looked pale and Casey wondered if she might throw up. She knew that feeling and couldn't help but feel sorry for the stupid girl.

"So," McAfee continued. "Would you like to make a little deal?"

Shelby looked up at him.

"I'm not a cop anymore but I've still got plenty of juice and I'm willing to help you out a bit if you're willing to play straight with us."

Shelby wiped the tears away with her palms and nodded.

"Good, let's talk about the night Jeremy was killed over there in that barn."

No more than five miles away FBI agents walked into the Jefferson police department and placed Chief Willie Charles under arrest for felony assault, impeding a police investigation, and attempted felony destruction of evidence. Simultaneously, agents picked up Donny Charles from Jefferson High and grabbed Ted Lawson at his barber shop. Both faced identical charges to the Chief. Due to the obvious level of corruption the men would be transported back to the Atlanta field office for questioning before being transferred to County jail to await a bond hearing. The Jefferson County Sheriff had been notified and had taken control of the town's police department. In all likelihood, it would become a permanent sub-station of the Sheriff's office moving forward.

Douglas, and Cindy Denning, a photographer for the Atlanta Daily, had waited eagerly outside to catch a shot of the Chief in handcuffs. "Make it good Cindy, this is front page tomorrow morning."

"She nodded and was in position as the agents escorted the uniformed Chief from the building. They had of course taken his badge and gun and though Douglas had expected a defeated look he got just the opposite. The Chief looked angry and defiant, incensed that anyone would have the balls to charge him with a crime.

Douglas stepped forward. "Can I have a comment, Chief?"

"Fuck you boy!"

Douglas winked at him. "Perfect. Thanks."

A black, four door sedan pulled down the overgrown dirt drive and came to a stop just behind McAfee's car. A tall, official looking woman in dark suit and darker sunglasses climbed out and walked toward them. She buttoned her jacket as she approached, squaring her shoulders and nodded slightly to McAfee.

"This is Detective Johansen of the Jefferson County Sheriff's department," he said directly to Shelby. "She's going to listen and you're going to speak. The only question right now is whether you're off to jail on a murder charge today or just cutting a deal in exchange for testifying to all the pertinent facts."

"Before we begin I need to read you your rights," the Detective said. "You have the right to remain silent, anything you say can and will be held against you in a court of law. You have the right to legal counsel. If you cannot afford counsel a lawyer will be appointed to you by the judge. Do you understand these rights and if so do you wish to speak to me today?"

Shelby looked uncertain and turned to Casey. Casey sighed, understanding the fear and anxiety of the situation since she'd experienced it all personally. "She's only fifteen. Shouldn't her Mom be with her for this?"

"She's not under arrest at this time so it's not necessary," the Detective replied. "But she's welcome to go that route if she chooses, yes."

"Not under arrest yet," McAfee added. "Maybe that doesn't need to happen."

"Correct." Detective Johansen agreed. "But if we leave here in my car without coming to an understanding you will be charged with assault and tampering."

"It's all over, Shelby. Just fess up and tell them what you know."

"I didn't hurt anybody, I swear I didn't."

"Let's hear it," McAfee answered. "From the beginning. Tell us what happened to Jeremy."

Shelby nodded, looking resigned to her fate. "Okay."

Lots of places began to cool off by mid-September. Jefferson County Georgia was not one of them. Further up in The Blue Ridge, up where all the vacation spots and rafting outfitters were, you might be able to catch a refreshing breeze here and there but that was about it. Most years you'd break a sweat just walking out to your own mailbox, sometimes straight up through November. There was a lot going on at that time of year, cause even though Jefferson didn't have the mountain views and tourist traps they had two things that brought them their own fair share of visitor cash. Apples, and their proximity to Atlanta. If you were city folk in need of a day away from the hustle and bustle you could hop in your car and be in Jefferson in less than an hour. Jefferson, Smith's Grove, and Black River had all the same charm as Helen, Blue Ridge, or Mountain City without all the summer congestion and over-priced boutiques. People could come for the day, pick some apples, have a picnic, or browse some of the vintage shops or local art galleries, and still make it back home in time for supper. But it was hot, that was for sure. Hot enough that many folks just flew right past on their way up to go inner-tubing in the mountains.

There were the festivals and holiday celebrations as well. Always supportive of local flavor and tradition while designed to bring in visitors with cash burning holes in their pockets. The fourth of July was huge, Labor day as well, and the planning for the harvest festival, Christmas fair and Spring fling always began many months in advance. What seemed to visitors to be a casual, laid-back and easy going small town affair, was actually a well orchestrated, mapped out, and often well-scripted presentation that involved everyone from the fire Marshal to town planners and of course, every single member of the woman's club. The result was an engaging, enjoyable and profitable experience for all involved.

Marcus had been preparing for the Harvest festival since July. His husband had suggested that he get in on a little of the tourist action himself and sell some keepsakes and baked goods out in front of his floral shop. He'd decided on a mixture of Halloween and Christmas ornaments, hand painted by some volunteers at an animal rights organization in the city. The purchase helped them to do their important work while leaving enough of a margin for him to make a tidy profit. Between the ornaments and his mother's ginger-bread recipe he hoped to have a thousand- dollar day. Perfect timing just before the holiday season.

Marcus had put Jeremy to work sorting the ornaments by style and price. Clay needed to be sorted from glass and ceramic, and all of them needed colorful ribbon in either orange or green for Halloween or Christmas. Each needed to be priced with a small white tag and then carefully placed in the display trays he'd fashioned from some leftover styrofoam packing material that he'd sprayed cheerful colors. The festival was still over a month away but there was still the standard seasonal stock to be rotated in, as well as fall decorating and Halloween lighting. The gingerbread baking would begin two weeks before the festival and on top of all that there were plenty of floral orders for weddings, events and parties to keep up with. Marcus was grateful for the extra help and Jeremy was always eager to work.

Jeremy had been distant the last few days and Marcus knew without asking that things weren't great in school. High School was treacherous for even the strongest and most popular kids but for a gay kid like Jeremy, with his slight build and quiet manner to boot, it could be traumatizing to say the least. He was quiet and shy, reserved, quite awkward actually if Marcus was being honest. The combination made Jeremy an instant target well before the issue of his sexuality was even considered. But in a small southern town like Jefferson, where the High School jocks were the kings of the realm, Jeremy's safety was a very real concern.

Marcus made his way over to the crafting table where Jeremy was working and pretended to check the ribbon stock on the spools. Jeremy stayed focused on his tasks and kept his head down. The boy could be intense, that was for sure. His dark eyes rarely revealing much emotion but his defeated slumping told the whole story.

"So," Marcus began casually. "What's good in the hood?"

Jeremy couldn't help but smile a little. "Do people actually say that?"

"Uh, I just did so yeah, it's a thing."

"You are the coolest guy I know."

"Back at you, homie."

Jeremy laughed and Marcus seized the opportunity.

"How are things in school? Jeremy cut off a small length of orange ribbon and shrugged. "Sucks."

Marcus nodded. He knew the pain all too well. "I used to find a quiet spot outside where I could eat my lunch without having to deal with anybody's bullshit."

Jeremy looked up. "You got picked on?"

"Oh shit yeah. You think it's tough being gay in the south now? Try twenty years ago. I never even came out either. They just assumed they knew and that's all it took man. Every kid that didn't wanna throw a football or chug beer till they passed out was a fag. One time some of the football players paid a girl to walk up to me and offer me oral just to see if I'd accept. I shoulda let that bitch do it."

Jeremy laughed. "What did you say?"

"I told her I didn't want whatever nasty ass diseases she was carrying."

"I told everybody. I dunno, I guess that was stupid."

Marcus placed his hand on Jeremy's shoulder. "It's never stupid to be yourself kid. Look, if you can find a way to blend, just to get through it all, then blend. That's my advice. Go to the games, cheer like an idiot, try to hang out with a few of the guys who maybe aren't such dicks. Maybe venture out to one or two of the safer parties. If you cower...even show a moment of fear, their bullshit will be relentless."

It was a little past five when the bell rang over the shop door and Emily entered with Shelby right on her heels. "My sister's here, Marcus. We're supposed to pick up some yellow squash and stuff for my Mom and meet up with her in front of the church."

"Okay buddy. Same time tomorrow?"

"I'll be here."

Jeremy walked out to the main room and nodded to his twin and Shelby.

"We gotta skedadle, Jeremy. Mama wants the veggies from Smith's but she wants the cream from the convenience store on account of it's fresher and she likes that brand better."

Jeremy nodded. "Looks like it's gonna let go y'all." He gazed out the front window at the darkening sky.

Emily frowned. "Then let's move out cause I just did my hair and I'd rather not end up looking like a wet rat."

"Cute apron," Shelby remarked and Jeremy realized he'd forgotten to take it off in the back. He pulled it over his head and folded it neatly on the counter. "See ya Marcus."

"Alright now," he called from the back. "Y'all be good."

Smith's was never crowded but it looked fairly busy for a weekday. It was just about five-fifteen when the three of them entered and Emily grabbed a basket. "Yellow squash, canned pineapple, crushed almonds and two tomatoes," she announced. "Jeremy, you get the nuts and pineapple and I'll hit the produce aisle. I wanna make it to the convenience store and back to the church before it starts spittin'."

He nodded silently and headed for the canned fruit section. He never minded that Emily was more assertive than he. She had always been a little bossy and claimed to be his big sister since she was born four minutes before him. He never minded her taking the lead though, in fact, he kinda liked it. He never detected any meanness in it and since he preferred to keep to himself anyway it made sense to let his sister do the talking. Emily liked to plan and organize and delegate. Jeremy preferred to observe, hang back, and quietly do as he was asked.

He quickly found the canned pineapple and the bags of nuts were hanging at the end of the same isle. As he rounded the corner to head back toward the produce section he spotted his sister and Shelby talking with Shelby's brother Danny and his buddies Mike and Jessie. He slowed his walk as much as possible, hoping to avoid the inbreds. But their conversation seemed to be continuing so eventually he was dropping the items he'd picked up into Emily's cart. The other boys looked at him with disgust and had it not been for the presence of the two girls he knew they'd be shoving him around already. Danny smiled wryly at Emily. "And bring Jeremy along with you. He needs to stop acting better than the rest of us and start chillin' with everybody else."

Emily glanced quickly toward her brother, then back to Danny. "He doesn't like parties and stuff."

"Come on now," Danny turned to Jeremy. "We're all gonna chill tonight man. Just fuckin' come and lets bury all the dumb shit once and for all."

Jeremy turned to his twin sister who had the ability to read his every thought.

"Maybe," she said. "We'll see what happens. We gotta go, my Mama's gonna spit fire if we keep her waiting."

"Alright then," Danny smiled. "I know my sis is comin'. I know you never turn down a couple cold ones."

Shelby grinned. "Just make sure your boyfriends all keep their hands off me."

"They fuckin' know better."

The boys walked off and Jeremy nudged his sister. "What was that about?"

They gonna have a party out at the Jessler barn. Sounds like just twenty people or so. Drink a few beers is all."

"What's that got to me with me?"

"My brother's prolly tryin' to get in your sisters pants," Shelby teased. "So he's bein' nice to you so you don't convince her to steer clear."

"Ain't nobody gettin' in my damn pants Shelby. And you shouldn't be lettin' none of them morons touch you either."

"I dunno. Jessie's kinda cute."

"Jessie's a dipshit that can barely spell his own name. You can do a whole lot better."

"But what's it have to do with me?" Jeremy asked again.

"I don't know Jeremy," Emily sighed. "But he's right you know. If you'd just try to fit in a bit with some of the other boys life would get much easier for you. I don't like watchin' you have to tolerate their bullshit."

"Just come," Shelby added. "You can sit right next to me Jeremy."

"Good idea. Keep those two legged cockroaches away from her," Emily winked.

They grabbed the squash and tomatoes and headed up front to pay. They'd have to rush now to avoid their Mama's wrath.

Nobody made dinner in the Timmons home except Carla Timmons. Emily had become a good cook in her own right, learning all she could from her experienced, and award-winning, Mama. She was allowed to prepare lunches and even do her part for holiday meals and baking, but her Mama would not relinquish control of dinner preparation. She saw it as her duty as a mother, wife and homemaker, a proper country southern belle who took everything from napkin folding to throw pillows with equal measure of importance. Dinner was more than a quick fix, it was tradition. There was no eating in front of the TV, or eat and run, at the Timmons house. All four family members were expected to be seated at the table and enjoy the meal they'd been blessed with. Guests were fine as long as they knew the rules and minded their manners, like sweet Miss Shelby. Carla loved that girl to the moon and back. She and her Emily had been friends since they were in diapers and the two of them had always stuck together like glue.

Tonight was pot roast night. Cooked to perfection, as usual, with baby carrots and the little red potatoes that everybody loved so much. She baked a beautiful apple pie just this morning and hand whipped her own cream for the topping. The five of them sat around the table laughing and talking about their day. Since it was Friday the kids weren't in any rush to get homework done. The rule was that it needed to be finished by seven on Sunday evening. If you chose to get it out of the way right after school on Friday then great, if not, pick your time. Just don't complain about it after you've made your choice.

The girls were giggling about some secret or other as her husband launched into a story about how he'd twisted a rod on the tractor and was mad at himself for trying to pull out a stump without the truck. "Damned thing keeps given' me shit," he growled.

"Language, Roy."

"Sorry. It ain't like they don't hear it all day long in school."

"Not at the dinner table they don't."

"Fine," he conceded.

Jeremy sat quietly, moving the last few bites of pie around with his fork and looking completely disinterested in his present company.

"How was school today?" she asked pointedly in his direction.

"It was fine, Mama."

"Anything exciting happen?"

He raised his eyes to acknowledge the question but lowered them again quickly. "No Ma'am."

His Dad shook his head and stood up to clear his plate. "Don't bother."

"Stop it Roy. That's not helping."

He walked off without a word, dropping off his dish in the sink and continuing right out the back door.

Carla stood up as well, grabbing her own plate and then Jeremy's, kissing the top of his head before walking back into the kitchen.

Emily waited till her mother was out of earshot before leaning across the table to whisper to her brother. "You're gonna come tonight?

"No."

"Come on. Maybe this is what you need to make some friends. Nothing bad's gonna happen. I'm gonna be right there with you."

"Me too," Shelby added as she ate her last bite of pie. "So good."

Emily reached her hand across the table and Jeremy rolled his eyes slightly before taking it in his.

"You know you can't say no to me little brother."

He found himself smiling, she was good at making him smile. "I really don't want to but if it's that important to you I'll come for a few minutes."

Emily got excited. "Yay!"

"Just a few minutes Emily. I mean it, okay?"

Their parents were always in bed by ten. Farm folks were always up before the dawn and they were no exception. Emily's Mama came in to kiss her and Shelby goodnight, finding the two girls in their jammies looking at some fashion website with way too skinny models. Jeremy was in his room sketching in his pad and looking sullen as always. She sat down beside him on the bed and he stopped to look at her. "Are you okay love?"

"I'm fine Mama."

"You know you can always talk to me about anything."

"Dad hates me."

His mother looked shocked. "No. No Jeremy. He just doesn't understand, honey."

"Do you?"

"Sweetie, okay, I can't say I understand but I'm trying and I love you no matter what."

"No matter what. You mean even if I'm an abomination."

"I never said that and never will."

"Other people say it."

"People like to hate, Jeremy. They find a little nugget of something and grasp onto it as justification to be ugly to others. Usually it's because their own lives are so empty and disappointing that they need to lash out at others."

"But they say the Bible…"

"I know what the Bible says. I've been readin' it all my life and I know all about what the Old Testament says. I'm choosing to worry about what Jesus said and that's what I'm suggesting you do as well. And Jesus ain't said nothing about name calling, hating, abusing, pointing fingers, laughing, ridiculing or generally being a dumbass."

Jeremy smiled. "Yes Ma'am."

"And let your Daddy worry about himself. If he wants to act like a schoolboy and jump whenever the likes of Ted Lawson or Willie Charles say boo then so be it. That don't need to be of any concern to you."

"Okay Mama."

She kissed him and touched his cheek. "Okay. Sleep tight my love."

She was barely out the bedroom door when Emily and Shelby slipped in. "Damn Jeremy, what the hell were you talkin' about for so long?"

"Nuthin'," he shrugged.

"I was fixin' to leave your ass."

"You shoulda."

"Nope. I knew that's what you were tryin'. You said you're coming and that's that."

"Fine, let's go."

"Um, you know you're not wearing that shirt."

He glanced in the mirror. "What's wrong with it? It's a barn."

She shook her head. "Boys. A t-shirt is fine. Just please find one that don't look like you jus' wiped your ass with it please."

He took another look in the mirror and shrugged. Shelby grinned and opened up his dresser. "This one's cute."

He took it without a word and changed quickly before following the two girls out into the hallway and down the steps.

Marvin Jessler was a kindly old man who had been born on his family's cotton farm eighty-seven years ago. He had married the love of his life, Madeleine, sixty-four years ago and the two had managed the operations of the farm ever since. They had four grown sons and three daughters, seventeen grandchildren, eight great-grandchildren, four german shepherds, six goats, three cats and a parrot that often quoted Scripture. Their family had been in Jefferson going on two hundred years, most of it right there on the same patch of cotton they relied on today. Marvin was one of the most respected town leaders, descendant of Thomas Jessler, one of the town founders and brother-in-law to Hornton Jefferson after whom the town was named. The entire family was always well liked and highly regarded and Madeleine made apple fritters that could make a grown man cry. The best part about the Jesslers was that they went to bed about eight o'clock and you could party all night in their old barn without them even stirring.

Emily, Shelby and Jeremy arrived at ten-forty, the walk from the Timmons house only taking about fifteen minutes. It was a paved road but a little treacherous at night in the pitch darkness and while trying to navigate the potholes. The cotton fields were wide open in all directions so at least you didn't have to worry about bears or anything jumping out and killing you. What the girls did need to worry about was drunken boys who were hornier than they were smart. Out here in the open country you could scream bloody murder and nobody would hear. Emily was glad that her brother had agreed to come along for the walk.

About seventeen to twenty kids had gathered, fifteen of them boys. At least with Danny Lawson there none of them would get out of line with his sister or Emily. Jeremy might be another matter, being as Danny was the ultimate bully. Emily hoped that for tonight they would all lay off and just try and have a good time. Maybe they might even give her brother a chance and they'd find out he was actually a very sweet guy. She knew him for who he really was. A talented, artistic, funny and loyal kid who would do anything to help anybody. Sometimes she'd find herself just wanting to be completely separated from him. As much as she loved him he'd gone and made his damn announcement and now his unpopularity was somehow reflected onto her and lots of kids she used to be friendly with shunned her like some kinda leper. It wasn't fair that his choices were used to judge her, twins or not, and she couldn't help resenting him for it at times. Still, she loved him. They were twins and there was an undeniable connection between them and when he was sad it made her want to cry herself. She hoped that tonight might prove to be the change in the tide she'd been praying for.

Danny spotted them as they entered the lantern-lit space and walked over to greet them. He nodded first to

Shelby, "Dork," before giving Emily a slight hug. He reached out his hand to Jeremy who accepted it cautiously. "Glad you came Timmons. It's about time you chilled with us."

Jeremy offered a tight smile and Danny returned it. "Beer! Let me get y'all some beers."

There were three full coolers of nothing but beer and ice, a whole lot for a relatively small group especially since the girls tended to stick with one or two. Emily was friendly with several of the other girls, good friends with one of them. Shelby, of course, was friends with everybody. All of the boys liked her too, though they were especially careful with Danny around cause if he thought for a moment you were scoping out his baby sister he'd beat you till you cried out for your Mama. He teased her, tormented her, called her names, but never once laid so much as a finger tip on her. He clearly loved her, but he'd never admit it even if you tortured him.

All of Danny's friends were there. The jock mob as Jeremy liked to call them. Ronnie, Mike, Jessie, even Donny Charles. Shelby wondered what the Chief would say if he knew his son was out there chugging beer and acting the fool. Chief Willie never seemed like a guy to go for this sort of thing. When she'd see him she always imagined that he had an actual stick embedded up his ass. Her Daddy said that's what made him a good police Chief. Good old fashioned common sense and his zero tolerance for pretty much anything that was fun.

The Jessler's hadn't used this barn for more than twenty years. Even then it was more of a storage building for old tools and spare parts for some of the machinery. It was stable enough to hang out in but you probably wouldn't wanna choose it to ride out a storm. Jeremy was studying the old ceiling beams when Danny approached him and handed him a can of Budweiser. "Imagine putting those things up there by hand back in the day. They used to have like four guys hoist them up on their shoulders and just walk up fuckin' ladders and secure them in place. Those ol' boys didn't need gym memberships."

Jeremy grinned. "I s'pose not."

"That's why this place is still standing. I'm thinking about asking Mister Jessler if I can use it to work on some old trucks. Restoring them and painting them an' all. I could even drape plastic and create a dust free paint booth."

Jeremy nodded. "That's a good idea. Have you done it before?"

"Helping my Dad out and stuff. But you know, a cheap old truck, maybe five hundred bucks, get it purring like a kitten and all shined up. It'd be awesome."

"That would be pretty cool. Get your own business going an' all."

"Right?"

The two boys sipped their beer and watched some of the girls dance to a Travis Tritt song. Danny placed his hand on Jeremy's shoulder for a moment. "Hey, listen man, I know I've been a dick. Sorry about all that. We're all glad you came though. We all need to grow up and get along. It's like you said, if I'm fixin' to be a businessman right?"

Jeremy smiled, a bit of relief washing over him. He'd been dreading coming here since the market earlier. His anxiety level had been at an all time high since dinner, screaming inside his brain to stay in his room and take cover. They had shown him nothing but loathing since the end of last year. He'd wished he'd never come out, both for his own sake and for Emily's. Even his Dad seemed repulsed by him, he handn't hugged him or even touched him since he'd come out to them and told them he was gay. His Dad had gotten up from the sofa and walked out the back door and had barely communicated with him since then. He used to always invite him back to his workshop to teach him stuff or show him some new gadget he'd created to help with one task or another. But now he seemed to just wanna steer clear and avoid any contact with his son. As if Jeremy had some disease that he'd catch just by being in the same room as him.

School had been a never-ending nightmare that he couldn't seem to wake up from. One group of boys, most

210

of them present in the barn with him right now, had led the entire school in a campaign designed to inflict as much heartache, embarrassment and ridicule on Jeremy as they possibly could. But suddenly the tide seemed to be changing. The guys had all nodded to him, patted him on the back even. As Danny went on and on about candy apple red paint jobs, dual exhausts and lift kits, Jeremy found himself almost feeling foolish. Had it all just been in fun? Just boys being boys, messin' with one of their own that they'd know their whole lives? They almost seemed as if they'd be surprised to learn how he'd felt. Like he was as much one of them as any of the others. Had he gotten it all so terribly wrong? Was he just supposed to have manned up and laughed it off with the rest of them? Returned the jabs and enjoyed the good-natured fun?

One beer turned to two, three, four. Emily and Shelby had been dancing until they were clearly too drunk to dance any more. Some of the boys began to look as if they were eyeing their prey and Jeremy mentioned as much to Danny who called out to Mike. "Yo dude, you said you're heading out soon?"

"Yeah, man. I gotta be up at five to go fishin' with my Dad and Pops."

"Alright, cool. Do me a solid and drop my sister and Emily back home on your way."

"No problem. They both goin' to your house?"

"Fuck no. My Dad would kill us all. Jus' bring them down the street to Emily's."

"Cool. You comin' Jeremy?"

"Naw," Danny answered for him. "He's chillin' with me tonight. I'll bring him home myself later on. That cool with you man?" He turned to Jeremy and smiled.

Jeremy nodded. "Yeah. That's cool with me."

Emily took Jeremy by the hand and pulled him out of earshot. "Are you okay? You don't have to stay. Just come home with us."

"I'll be okay. It's like you said I need to hang out with them a little and maybe they'll start to like me. Everybody's been really cool all night."

"What about the first day of school? What they did to you?"

Jeremy closed his eyes for a second. "I dunno. I really don't know who did what. But I need to live here Em. We both do. Maybe if I try then they will too."

She looked completely unconvinced and shook her head. "No. This was a good first step but just come home with me."

Jeremy smiled. "You're slurring your words. Don't wake up Mama and Daddy or they'll whoop all our asses."

"Please just come home with me."

He kissed his sister's cheek. "Seriously, I'll be fine. They want me to be one of the boys right? So here I am being one of the boys."

Shelby and Emily followed Mike out the door and the other girls seemed to take that as their cue to beat it out of Dodge. There were too many drunken boys for a couple of drunk girls to possibly feel safe with. After a short while it was Jeremy, Danny, Donny Charles, Ron and Jessie. Ron produced a set of throwing knives and the boys took turns aiming for a chalk target that Jessie had sketched out on the wall. When Jeremy's turn came he decided to play along and give it a shot.

"Hold it by the blade, let the weight of the handle propel it," Danny coached.

Jeremy's three throws all bounced off into the dirt.

"Not bad," Danny encouraged him. "It's all in the wrist. Just loosen up in the wrist a bit more."

"Should be easy for you to be loose in the wrist," Jessie jabbed.

Jeremy laughed it off and the other guys did too. Maybe that was the key after all. Let them have their stupid little jokes and send a few back their own way. Boys just being boys.

They drank a little more beer and kept taking turns throwing the knives until they got bored. Jeremy had actually been pleased to get three in a row to stick close to the center of the target. The other guys had grunted their approval and he found himself actually feeling accepted for the first time in a long while. Truthfully, he'd never really felt all that comfortable around other guys ever. He'd always preferred to just hang out with Emily and her friends, at least until they began to make it clear that the old arrangement wasn't going to cut it in middle school and beyond. They weren't little kids anymore and the girls wanted to talk privately with their friends without a boy listening in. He got it. He didn't like it but he understood. The hard part was that it left him out on his own, uncomfortable with the other boys but not always welcome with the girls. It wasn't like he wanted to play dress up or anything. He'd heard that some people were born transgender and felt trapped inside of the wrong body. Jeremy was perfectly comfortable in his own skin. He never wanted to be a girl or act like a girl, he just found himself attracted to guys. Not these assholes but other guys. Maybe that's what he needed to do. Make it clear that he had no intention or desire to try to do anything with any of them. Could be they just needed to hear that.

"I'm done with this," Danny announced. The others nodded their agreement.

"Let's grab a couple more cold ones and hang out in the loft. You guys can help me decide on a layout for my restoration business."

They raised the old ladder up and steadied it against the floor of the loft. Ron tested it to make sure it was solid and put his unopened can of beer in his back pocket to make the climb up. The others followed and all took their seat along the edge looking down over the wide open space.

"It looks so much higher from up here," Jeremy remarked.

"Right," Danny answered. "High enough for a manual lift right Jess?"

Jessie nodded. "No doubt. The beams look nice and solid still so I wouldn't worry about a motor hoist either."

They sat in silence for a little bit, sipping their beer and surveying the space from above.

"This would be a cool place for a Halloween party," Jeremy said.

"Oh hell yeah," Danny laughed. "We probably have enough time to pull that together still."

The others all agreed and began to talk about ways to scare the living hell out of unsuspecting party goers. Ron suggested even scattering scarecrows out in the field surrounding the barn. Just close enough to be menacing but not so close that you could be sure those fuckers weren't actually alive.

"So, Jeremy," Danny changed the subject. "Shit's been pretty messed up this year man. I guess we were all just surprised you know?"

Jeremy nodded but kept his mouth shut to see where this was going.

"I mean, where did all this fag shit come from? I mean, gay shit or whatever?"

Jeremy had gone from being very comfortable to not at all comfortable in seconds. The tone has suddenly changed, the air seemed to get sucked out of the space very quickly and he found himself noticing little things like the smell of the moldy old wood and the creaking sound the doors made as they swayed back and forth in the breeze. He felt as if all eyes were on him, even though nobody was actually looking his way. But they were all focused on him, he knew it as surely as he knew he wasn't as safe as he'd thought he was. There was something unseen slowly closing in around him, menacing and heavy. He felt his chest tighten up a bit and began to notice his own breathing getting heavier and heavier. He was certain that they all noticed it too. There was no more laughing, no more joking around or taking light jabs at one another. He noticed how the lantern light seemed dimmer than it had earlier, casting shadows onto the dark wall boards and making him sorry he'd mentioned Halloween cause now he felt scared to death.

Jessie rubbed his legs. "I gotta stretch. Coach fucked me up making me run those laps." He shoved himself back and up onto his feet with a grunt.

"Serves you right being that late to practice, bitch," Danny answered.

The other boys all laughed and Jeremy was more than grateful for the change in subject. It wasn't a big deal, he told himself. See, they went from you to Jessie without missing a beat. It's just what guys do when they're hanging out together. He should leave it right there, he thought, but felt somehow compelled to let them know that he had no thoughts at all about any of them. They had no reason to ever feel uncomfortable around him ever.

"Hey guys, y'all know that I've never thought about any of you or any other guy in school like that, right?"

Nobody answered for a few minutes. That's good, he thought, maybe it's sinking in and they're realizing that they've been overreacting to the whole situation. Sure, if a straight guy thinks another guy is checking him out in the showers after gym class it might freak him out. He got it. But now they know it's not like that and they can all move on and be cool about it. People are different. Some are artistic and some analytic. Some athletic and some clumsy and awkward. Some are gay and some are straight. They were more alike than they were different. Raised in the same small Georgia town with the same values and traditions. They all attended the same churches, knew each other's families, shared a common community history.

It surprised him at first when Danny looped his arm through his and pulled him tightly to him. It was a date move wasn't it? Like when you stroll through the park with somebody or walked to your car after seeing a movie. He was startled by the, what...tenderness? Only for a split second until Ron did the same thing with his other arm. Only then did it register that he wasn't being supported or comforted, he was being restrained.

"You know what?" Danny said calmly. "You and I used to be friends, you remember?"

Fear gripped Jeremy and his mind began to race, wondering what they were planning, what to say. "Danny, I…"

"It's not your fault bud. Don't get upset over it. Nuthin' you can do to change it now."

"Danny please."

"Let's do this. I've known this kid all my life and don't wanna drag this out."

Jeremy was aware of Jessie moving up quickly behind him. He felt something being placed roughly around his neck, tightened. He watched in terror as Jessie threw the other end of the rope up and over the closest beam. He and Donny made their way down the ladder and took hold of the end tightly. Jeremy's tears came now, urgently but unashamedly. He knew this was the end. There would be no talking his way out of it, no reasoning with the hatefulness that was driving their actions. Just the same, he turned to Danny and attempted one last plea. "You don't have to do this, Danny."

Danny locked eyes with him and paused for just a second. "I'm sorry bud, but I do."

Jeremy felt Danny's hand press firmly against his back. He found it oddly comforting until Danny shoved him off the edge.

Casey wasn't a hardened cop like McAfee or Detective Johansen and she didn't give a shit that tears were streaming down her face. She was more upset about the fact that Shelby's face was perfectly dry. Her voice was tense when she was finally able to speak. "How do you know all of this?"

"My brother called me. Getting the stories straight and all of that. He wanted me to say that I saw Jeremy come back into the house that night if anybody asked. And to tell Emily the same thing."

"And did you?"

"Yes. When we woke up I told her Jeremy had come into her room to make sure we were okay before he went to bed."

"What then?"

"I called my Dad."

"Was your Dad involved in the planning?"

"No. And he was in an absolute panic. He told me to stick with the story Danny told me and not to say another word. He said he'd take care of everything."

"So what did he do?"

"He called Chief Willie and a couple of the other men and they all came over to our house. They talked about what to do so the boys wouldn't have to go to prison the rest of their lives."

"Who was there?"

"My Dad, the Chief, Ron and Jessie's Dad's."

"Was Mike in on the plan? Was that his job to get you and Emily out of there?"

"I don't know. I never thought about it."

McAfee rubbed his temples and exchanged a glance with Detective Johansen.

"So, your statement is that these boys had planned this from the start. They knew what they were going to do well before the party started?"

"I really don't know, Sir. I just know what they did. But Emily and I had nothing to do with it I swear!"

"Well dear, maybe Emily didn't. But you're what we call an accessory after the fact. You knew about a murder, helped to cover your brother and the other boys, and let his family agonize without ever saying a word. In Georgia that's about fifteen years in prison."

Shelby began to cry again and Detective Johansen frowned. "You know what I'm noticing Shelby? When you're worried about yourself you start to get emotional but you told us all about poor Jeremy's terrifying ordeal and death without so much as a single tear. Detective McAfee is right, fifteen years for accessory but you went beyond that and became involved in a felony assault and attempting to destroy evidence. I'd say we're looking at fifteen to life."

She broke down sobbing and McAfee motioned for Casey to walk away with him. They moved back behind the cars and McAfee placed his hand on Casey's shoulder. "You okay?"

"How did you know they had murdered him?"

"Douglas and I had suspected from the start and we knew for sure when you were attacked. People don't panic like that just to cover up some bullying. Shelby's Dad and Willie and Donny got picked up this morning. Obviously more charges are coming. A lot more."

They walked back over and McAfee leaned against the front of Shelby's car.

"So, last question for right now. We know Donny Charles was one of the guys who attacked Casey. And I know who the other one was too. But go ahead and tell us anyway."

Shelby lowered her head and after a moment of quiet mumbled something inaudible into her chest.

"Louder," McAfee said.

Her anguish was apparent. Not for the poor kid who was mercilessly bullied and then killed, but for her own family. "It was my brother."

Week Seven

Casey ordered her usual, some chilli cheese fries and a large toffee milkshake. Emma and Tasha shook their heads and grinned.

"How do you stay so skinny girl?" Emma laughed.

"And she looks like she hits the gym every day when the truth is she lays on the sofa reading her books all day long," Tasha added.

"Don't hate," Casey smirked. "Appreciate."

"You're a nerd," Emma smiled.

"So you're caught up with your schoolwork?" Tasha asked her.

"Yeah. I never got too far behind. All my professors were really cool about it."

Emma took a bite of her turkey wrap. "Anything new on Jeremy's case?"

"They boys have all been charged with first degree murder. Their Dads were charged with accessory and Chief Willie has been charged with a bunch of stuff involving corruption. They added on felony assault for Donny Charles and Danny Lawson for attacking me."

"What about the little bitch?"

"Shelby took a deal to testify against everybody else and she'll plead guilty to a couple misdemeanors and do a couple years probation."

"You think she knew about any of it in advance?" Tasha asked.

"I don't think she knew about the murder in advance. I'm not sure about the attack on me."

The waitress cleared away their lunch plates and came back with a giant ice cream sundae that she deposited in front of Casey. The other girls began to laugh.

"Y'all shut up. I got three spoons."

She pushed the giant desert into the center of the table and they all dug in.

"Okay," Emma got serious. "I wanna talk about the big day."

"Y'all are like my adoption maids of honor," Casey smiled.

"Is that a thing?" Tasha laughed.

"It is if we say it is!"

"No matching dresses please," Emma scrunched up her nose.

"Oh hell no. Hair and nails though you guys. We'll all go together the morning of. Cool?"

Emma and Tasha nodded their agreement.

"What's up with Jerry?" Emma asked.

Casey shrugged and looked around the crowded Diner. "I dunno. Things are moving slowly forward so I guess we'll see."

"You and Douglas are heading out next week for thanksgiving in Savannah, right?"

"Sure are. You two still going home to Concord?"

"Yeah," Tasha reached over and touched Casey's hand. "Wish you were coming with us."

Casey smiled. "Too many bad memories. I need to leave all that way behind me. I'll tell you what though you guys, all my good memories from back then are because of you two and your families. I love you guys."

The three of them joined hands in the center of the table for a moment.

"Okay," Casey pulled free. "Ice cream's melting."

"Everything still set for tomorrow night?" Emma asked through a mouthful of ice cream.

"Yes. Y'all still riding up with us?"

The girls nodded.

"It's gonna be emotional," Emma said almost to herself.

Casey sighed. "Yeah. Yeah it is."

The evenings had begun to turn comfortably cooler. Casey enjoyed the refreshing breeze as she passed out candles to folks as they arrived and gathered by the Jessler's old barn. The couple had been kind enough to welcome the important vigil but had announced that circumstances being as they were, the structure would be torn down before Christmas. Some of the local residents had floated the idea of a permanent cross to be erected on site and the Jessler's gave their enthusiastic approval.

The girls had split up, Casey by the driveway with Emma and Tasha about twenty yards to either side of her. People parked along the roadway, arriving solo or in families, carrying teddy bears, balloons, flowers, and beautiful handmade signs offering prayers. They had been nervous about the turnout, wanting it to be a fitting memorial to the bravery of a young boy who fought a battle completely on his own in order to remain true to who he really was. There had been so many that were unwilling to accept him, hateful in fact, but tonight the others came forward. At first there were twenty, an acceptable number and one that Casey could have lived with. But then came another twenty, and another. Right now she'd put the number at about two hundred and growing by the minute. LGBTQ organizations out of Atlanta had put out the word and Douglas's front page story had connected with the emotions of thousands. Groups were arriving from the city in droves.

Casey saw Douglas off in the distance conducting interviews and directing the staff photographer. McAfee was supervising all the security volunteers, mostly retired Atlanta cops and local Sheriff's deputies. The turnout was already making her happy, but then the busses began to pull up. The first was a group of students from Central Atlanta High School, chaperoned by what she assumed to be a group of parents. The second was a charter bus up from Macon, hired by the Georgia civil rights coalition. Several vans followed from Atlanta Pride and Marietta Christian church. Then came McAfee's surprise, a group of bagpiper's from the Atlanta PD marching band. They had run out of candles before she knew it, and she estimated the crowd to be somewhere around fifteen hundred.

She saw Douglas approaching her through the crowd and it took away some of her nervousness.

"Casey, look at what you've done. This is amazing, kid."

She shook her head in disbelief. "I'm so happy Douglas. I just can't believe it."

"Look, I know you weren't expecting this much of a turnout. If you want me to do it I will."

She took a deep breath and shook her head. "No, I need to do this. Not just for him, you know?"

Douglas hugged her to him tightly and for a moment she wasn't sure he had any intention of letting go. But he finally gave one last bit of a squeeze and loosened his hold. "Go get 'em Casey."

She made her way through to the barn where McAfee was waiting for her by his pickup. He opened up the tailgate and helped her up into the bed of the truck. He handed her the microphone and showed her where the button was to turn it on.

"You're all plugged in." He winked at her. "You got this Malone."

She shot him a quick, nervous smile and flipped on the microphone.

"Hi everybody. Thank y'all for coming. Can you please come a little closer and gather around. Maybe all y'all without candles can use your phones and let's really light up this field."

The view from just over the heads of the crowd was truly beautiful. Flickering light that reached out to the edges of the cotton field and hovered over its pureness like sunrise on Christmas morning. It touched her heart and gave her hope for the world. If this many people would come out to celebrate one boy's life in the middle of nowhere then maybe there was truly genuine goodness out there. Because everybody gathered around her knew as well as her that this was about more than one solitary life. This was about decency and fairness. It was about your right to live your own life the way you choose and to do so without fear of being singled out and attacked. This was about teasing and bullying, hatefulness and evil. It was about watching what you say, guarding what you allow yourself to think, and keeping your damn hands to yourself.

Casey couldn't help but think back to when she was Jeremy's age. The trauma she endured at home would remain with her forever but somehow the words that other kids said to her were what continued to keep her awake at night till this day. She caught herself beginning to feel nervous again and suddenly noticed the silence of the crowd. She looked out over them, mostly strangers but everyone that she truly loved as well. Good friends too like Sammy, who'd taken a real chance on her and given her the opportunity of a lifetime to work for the Atlanta Daily. And Lloyd McAfee who worked twenty-four hours a day for two weeks straight to catch the guys who hurt her. Douglas was there, who'd become her father a while ago, judge's signature or no judge's signature. Emma and Tasha were there with their families and Jerry had shown up only moments before with bottles of water in case anybody needed some. She saw Emily and her parents right up front, heads low in both heartache and shame. Mister Timmons had been deflecting all along, lashing out at the school and the district, even his buddies in town for what he knew very well he was partly responsible for. The culture of hate he had spoken to Douglas and McAfee about at their first meeting was in large part his own creation and now the time had come to own that.

Marcus was there as well, arm in arm with a guy Casey assumed to be his husband. Marcus had become Jeremy's only friend. The only adult in a town full of familiar adults who paid any attention to a boy who was obviously at risk. Noticeably missing were the town's leaders. Lawson, Charles, Deen and Smith, as well as all the boys who'd been in the barn that night. Some in jail, others out on bond, all waiting to receive a punishment that would never be enough. Shelby and her Mom had beat it out of town, probably never to return. But as Douglas and Casey had driven through town earlier they'd passed beneath the banner announcing the annual Christmas fair and parade. Life goes on.

Casey raised the mic to her lips. "A few weeks ago I was told a story about Jeremy's eighth grade dance. It made me think back to when I was in the eighth grade and I remember very clearly when our own dance was approaching. I was never allowed to go to any of the dances or school activities like that. Most of them cost at least a few dollars and we were too poor for that sort of thing. It never bothered me all that much because I always preferred to be by myself anyway and read my books. I never had many friends, most of the time not any, and it suited me fine because I was happier as a loner. At least I convinced myself that was true.

Looking back now though, I can clearly see that my happiest times were when I did have a friend I could talk to and share things with. I had one great friend who I loved but she was bullied so badly she just couldn't go on any longer and took her own life. She and I had been constant victims of the kind of meanness that opens deep wounds and never lets them heal. I don't know what made us different because we seemed to be so much the same. But in the end she made a choice to surrender and I made a choice to fight. Neither of those choices was wrong...it's just one is so much more tragic than the other. I've been thinking about Paulina a lot lately the last few weeks. I wish she was still here with me. I guess since I'm talking about her she kinda is."

Casey swept her gaze across the faces of the crowd, settling on Douglas who gave the slightest nod of encouragement.

"So when the dance was approaching I knew I wouldn't be going. Not just because my parents wouldn't let me but because I'd be reminded by my classmates at least twenty times a day that I was far too ugly for anybody to ever ask me. The funny part was I knew it wasn't true. It was only painful because I knew they hated me so deeply that they'd say something like that. And here I am, eight years later, remembering it like it happened just this morning. That's the thing of it y'all. The thing I wanna say to you today. Nothing hurts more or lasts longer than words. I'm so lucky that I made some incredible friends later on in school and they're here today with me."

Casey looked down at Emma and Tasha but looked away quickly so that their teary expressions wouldn't get her started too. "But the new can bring happiness, and joy, and even peace. What it can't do is erase the damage that's already been done. All the people who love me now make my present life so incredible and my future so hopeful. But my past was still ugly. It'll stay ugly and it'll always be a part of me." She looked directly at Douglas. "I know my new Dad would take all that from me if he could. He's really tried. But he can't. But he's giving me this present life, and all the love he can possibly muster. It doesn't erase anything, but it does heal."

Casey reached down and took her candle from McAfee, holding it up in the air as others did the same. "There are lots of kids just like Jeremy in the world. And just like me. It's our responsibility to seek them out. It's our responsibility to step in and do something when we can, before it's too late. It's our responsibility to smile, and to say hello, and to offer a word of encouragement when we can. Jeremy was talented and smart and friendly. He was also very brave. I hope that the next time we see someone being that brave that we have at least enough courage to support them. But if not, hopefully we'll have the basic decency to keep our mouths shut."

McAfee helped her back down as the bagpipers began to play Amazing Grace. He hugged her around the shoulders in his bear sort of way. "Come with me for a minute."

She followed him over to where Emily stood with her parents, shaking hands and exchanging hugs with all those who came to offer condolences. They waited for a moment as a transgender woman talked to them about her own experiences with hatefullness and brutality. The disgust on Mister Timmons face probably seemed like a reaction to the story the woman was telling but Casey knew different. He didn't care about her suffering or if she thought about ending her own life. He just couldn't wait to break free from her, from all these repulsive freaks.

The woman offered her hand and Misses Timmons shook it politely. McAfee stepped forward with Casey right beside him. He nodded his head. "Folks."

Mister Timmons nodded back and Misses Timmons smiled tightly.

"Well, as you know, we've completed the investigation that you asked us to conduct. Clearly it went much deeper than you had first believed and I'm sure you're pleased about the arrests that have been made."

Misses Timmons nodded vigorously. "Oh, of course, very pleased that the truth has come out."

"Right, well, you asked us if the school was at fault for not protecting Jeremy. Our answer is yes. There is ample evidence that the school was aware of the bullying and harassment and did nothing to stop it. So, if you were to speak to an Attorney I'm sure you'd have a lawsuit."

Mister Timmons looked very pleased, but only for a moment.

"Of course, I'd make sure I was in court personally to testify as well Mister Timmons. To the hate and loathing you had for your own son and the fact that you, more than anyone else, damaged that poor child. I'll make good and goddamned certain you never see a single dime...because you're an absolute disgrace."

Emily hung her head as her father stood speechless, knowing full well every word was the truth.

McAfee stood looking at him for one more brief second. "Alright then."

He took Casey by the hand and led her back to Douglas.

Douglas took her in his arms and crushed her for the second time in only twenty minutes. "You were awesome, kid."

"I was nervous. Did I even make sense?"

"Gosh yes. Incredible. I'm proud of you."

She smiled and hugged him again. "I'm gonna go talk to everybody."

"Okay love."

She headed off and Douglas placed his hand on McAfee's shoulder. "You told them?"

"Oh yeah. They might win a case but if so we'll make sure that money goes to a prevention program or something. And we haven't even tried to dig up shit on that boy. I guarantee you there's a whole lot more."

"He was as much a part of the inner circle as any of them."

"Damn right he was."

"You did good on this one Lloyd. Really good. I feel like we did something important here."

"What say we get everybody together and grab a bite?"

"We are in the apple fritter capital of the world."

"Yessir. And now's our chance cause I've had enough of this town for a good long while."

Casey, Emma and Tasha sat side by side in luxurious salon chairs, enjoying the heating and massage elements while the attendants went about the business of their pedicures.

"So how was your hot date with Jerry last night?" Emma asked without opening her eyes.

"Really nice. He took me to a place downtown that I've seen great reviews on in the Daily. I told him he doesn't need to take me to such fancy places. It's too expensive."

"Hell, girl," Tasha replied. "If that boy wants to spend money on you then let him. He owes you that as an apology for running away."

"Like a little girl," Emma added.

Casey smiled. "You guys are so bad. He was just scared. And turns out he was right y'all. We were messing with murderers."

"Guess that makes us pretty damn badass," Emma grinned.

Casey laughed. "I guess it does."

"So where are you two gonna eat for Thanksgiving in Savannah?"

"We're staying at a really gorgeous old bed and breakfast in the historic district and the owners are cooking a big traditional dinner for all the guests. They've got a really beautiful brick patio and we're gonna eat out there."

"Wow," Tasha mumbled. "Wish I was going with y'all."

"Two weeks right?" Emma asked.

"Yup. We're gonna go see all the best spots for Christmas lights and even take a carriage ride or two."

Emma opened her eyes and took Casey's hand. "I can't believe he's actually gonna be your Dad."

"I know. And I'm so happy you guys are with me today."

"You couldn't keep us away."

"You got that right," Tasha added.

They moved over to the manicure station and admired the different polish colors they'd all chosen. Casey surprised herself, becoming suddenly emotional. She wiped away a tear but not before her friends saw it.

"Aww," Emma grabbed her in a tight squeeze and Tasha joined right in.

"Okay," Casey laughed and tried to breathe. "Y'all get off before you smudge my nails."

"ALL RISE!" The bailiff called the room to order. "THE ATLANTA DISTRICT FAMILY COURT IS NOW IN SESSION. THE HONORABLE NICOLE REDDINGTON PRESIDING."

Judge Reddington was a well known figure in the city. Her family was quite large, not to mention wealthy, and if there was a good cause to be found the Reddington's were usually sponsoring it. She had a tough job, being forced to separate more families than she joined. This room was where custody battles were waged, and abuse allegations were vetted. It was where neglectful foster families were held to account and where children were ordered to be taken away from their families and brought into the system. But on happier days, like today, it was where adoptions were finalized and new family bonds were established. Nicole Reddington lived for these days. "This is an adoption filing by Douglas Reginald Powell, seeking to adopt Miss Casey Bridget Malone, age twenty. Step forward please both of you."

Douglas and Casey walked hand in hand up to the bench as all of their friends looked on.

"Miss Malone, is it your desire to be adopted by Mister Powell today?"

"Casey smiled widely. "Yes your honor."

"Mister Powell, I assume it is still your desire to proceed with the adoption of Miss Malone?"

"Very much so, your honor." He put his arm around Casey and pulled her into him and the Judge smiled. "Normally I ask for character witnesses to come forward in adoption proceedings," she smiled. "Would anyone like to speak to Mister Powell's character?"

McAfee stood up, looking sharp in a new suit and his tie was actually fully tied.

"He's a character alright, your honor!"

Everyone laughed, including judge Reddington. "You be quiet there Lloyd."

Douglas turned and grinned at his friend for a moment.

"Well," the judge continued, "Since I've known Mister Powell for more than twenty years I will vouch for him personally as well. He's a man of great integrity and a valuable member of the Atlanta community. I'm approving your petition and it's my pleasure to announce that you are now legally father and daughter."

Casey grabbed Douglas tightly as everyone rushed forward to congratulate them. Judge Redington stayed to take a few selfies with them and pulled Casey aside for a brief moment. "I'm familiar with who you are Casey and how much you've suffered. I just wanted you to know how very pleased I am to be a part of this today."

"Thank you so much, your honor."

"Are you in school?"

"Yes Ma'am. Second year."

"That's very good to hear. What's your major?"

"Journalism, Ma'am. I'm a bit limited on what I can do because of the felony record."

"From what I know of the case, that's a travesty. You should have walked away free and clear."

"Thank you, your honor. I'm happy to just be able to live a normal life."

"There must be things you'd like to do but can't with that hanging over your head."

"A bunch. But still, I'm grateful. Especially today." She glanced over toward Douglas and the judge reached out to shake her hand. "Go be with your Dad. But when you graduate Casey, you call me. The Governor will answer when I call, and we're going to see about fixing this matter the way it should have been to begin with."

Casey's face lit up. "Thank you so much! Can I hug you?"

The judge gave her a hug and patted her on the back. "Keep doing good in the world young lady."

"Yes Ma'am."

She walked back to Douglas and he took her hand. "What did the judge have to say?"

"That she's going to help me get my record completely cleared when I graduate."

Douglas looked excited. "Casey, that's huge!"

"It's a perfect day," she answered, and kissed his cheek. She looked up at him and smiled. "Dad."

Douglas pulled her back in and everyone applauded.

"Okay, let's go!" McAfee called out. "We're all hungry!"

They made their way out of the court building to head for the party, still shaking hands and accepting congratulations. Sammy came up between the two of them and put her arms around their waists. "Congratulations to both of you. This is a really awesome day."

"Thanks Sammy," Douglas answered. "It means a lot to both of us that you're here."

"Wouldn't miss it. So listen, when are you leaving for Savannah?"

"Two days," Casey answered.

"Hmm."

"What?" Douglas grinned. "I know that hmm. What's up?"

"Just say no if you want guys. I'll completely understand. We've got a reliable source that's giving us information on the sex trafficking of minors to big shots around the State but their base seems to be in Savannah."

"Good God," Douglas stopped walking and looked at her. "What about law enforcement?"

"A brick wall so far. These are apparently some powerful boys, Douglas. Nobody's touching this thing. I thought maybe you two might wanna poke around just a little bit and interview our source?"

Douglas and Casey looked at each other for a brief moment and smiled.

"Hey, Lloyd!" Douglas called out for McAfee.

McAfee turned around. "Yeah?"

"Wanna meet up with us in Savannah after thanksgiving and look into some pedophiles?"

McAfee nodded. "I'm in, brother. I'm all in."

Casey and Emma held hands as they headed for the cars.

"I'm so happy for you Casey."

"Me too Em. Thank you again for always being here for me."

"Always my peach. You know that."

They walked for just another moment in silence before Emma hugged Casey close to her. "Are you okay? I know you saw her too."

Casey nodded and squeezed Emma back. "Yeah, I'm perfect."

She stopped for a moment and looked across the parking lot at the woman who stood alone, watching them. The woman smiled slightly and nodded. Casey smiled back. "Bye Mama."

Follow Author B. Benedict Braddock on facebook and watch for the third book in the Douglas Powell/Casey Malone series, "Savannah," coming soon.